"You need to ge
"We're getting m

"What?" She backed up. "We are not."

"Correct me if I'm wrong, but I think you're a virgin because you made a conscious decision to wait for marriage. Right or wrong?"

"Right, but—"

"Then we're getting married." He opened his closet door.

"You can't just tell me we're getting married and expect me to obey, Michael Fortune."

He aimed a steady, fierce look at her, one that said, *Don't lie to me.* "Why did you decide to sleep with me, Felicity?"

"Because you're the one," she fired back.

"What does that mean?"

"I never wanted anyone before you, not enough to actually do it. You think it was hard to stay a virgin all these years? It wasn't. But you're different."

"How? Tell me exactly how."

"Because I'm in love with you."

He turned his head away so fast, she didn't get to see his reaction. "Then it's settled. Go get ready."

Dear Reader,

"Like a kid in a candy store" is the perfect description of my hero, Michael Fortune, when he first meets Felicity Thomas. Michael *is* like a kid in a candy store— *hers*. Felicity is a confectioner by trade—and a sweet confection to the usually cool and controlled Michael. For the Atlanta-born-and-raised man, the fact that her shop is in the quaint little town of Red Rock, Texas, is the best reason to avoid falling in love.

However, the sweet Felicity tempts big-city Michael, who, in turn, shows Felicity how different life could be for the small-town woman. But are their geographical differences an insurmountable barrier? Is love enough to conquer all?

I hope you enjoy the path their journey takes to sweet surrender.

Susan Crosby

A DATE WITH FORTUNE

SUSAN CROSBY

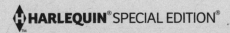

HARLEQUIN® SPECIAL EDITION®

Special thanks and acknowledgment to Susan Crosby for her contribution to the Fortunes of Texas: Southern Invasion continuity.

Recycling programs
for this product may
not exist in your area.

ISBN-13: 978-0-373-65721-6

A DATE WITH FORTUNE

HARLEQUIN®
www.Harlequin.com

Printed in U.S.A.

Books by Susan Crosby

Harlequin Special Edition

*The Bachelor's Stand-In Wife #1912
††*The Rancher's Surprise Marriage* #1922
*The Single Dad's Virgin Wife #1930
*The Millionaire's Christmas Wife #1936
†*The Pregnant Bride Wore White* #1995
†*Love and the Single Dad* #2019
§*The Doctor's Pregnant Bride?* #2030
†*At Long Last, a Bride* #2043
‡*Mendoza's Return* #2102
*Husband for Hire #2118
*His Temporary Live-in Wife #2138
*Almost a Christmas Bride #2157
§§*Fortune's Hero* #2181
‡‡*A Date with Fortune* #2239

**Wives for Hire
†The McCoys of Chance City
***Behind Closed Doors
††Back in Business
§The Baby Chase
‡The Fortunes of Texas:
    Lost…and Found
§§The Fortunes of Texas:
    Whirlwind Romance
‡‡The Fortunes of Texas:
    Southern Invasion

Other titles by this author
available in ebook format.

Silhouette Desire

**Christmas Bonus, Strings Attached #1554
**Private Indiscretions #1570
**Hot Contact #1590
**Rules of Attraction #1647
**Heart of the Raven #1653
**Secrets of Paternity #1659
The Forbidden Twin #1717
Forced to the Altar #1733
Bound by the Baby #1797

SUSAN CROSBY

believes in the value of setting goals, but also in the magic of making wishes, which often do come true—as long as she works hard enough. Along life's journey she's done a lot of the usual things—married, had children, attended college a little later than the average coed and earned a B.A. in English. Then she dove off the deep end into a full-time writing career, a wish come true.

Susan enjoys writing about people who take a chance on love, sometimes against all odds. She loves warm, strong heroes and good-hearted, self-reliant heroines, and she will always believe in happily-ever-after.

More can be learned about her at www.susancrosby.com.

To my new neighbors, who are already dear friends—
Nancy, Pat and Leo. You were an unexpected
and much appreciated bonus.

Chapter One

Michael Fortune walked into the 1950s-era diner, Estelle's, thinking it was like everything else in Red Rock, Texas—quaint. Michael didn't do quaint, which was probably the reason his cousin had chosen this place for lunch. To put Michael off his A game. The place was a living, breathing piece of nostalgia with its long Formica counter, red leatherette booths and chrome-legged tables and chairs.

He took a seat in an empty booth, and a few minutes later a fiftyish woman set a glass of water on the tabletop, next to his cell phone.

"Sorry to keep you waiting, honey. My name's Estelle," she said, sticking the eraser of her pencil against the back of his hand, stopping his fingers from drumming on the table. "I can see you're the impatient type."

"So my family tells me."

"You're new in town," Estelle said. "Must be meeting someone."

The town gossip, Michael decided. "My cousin Wyatt and his fiancée. I'm early, though."

"Ahh. You're a Fortune, then. They sure do grow 'em handsome in Atlanta." She cocked a hip and settled her gaze on him. "Good men, your cousins. It was pretty big news around here when they packed up and settled down in Red Rock."

Which was the very reason he'd come to Texas. Michael's uncle James had begged him to intervene. "Talk some sense into that son of mine," his uncle had said, frustrated at Wyatt's—and his three other sons'—defection from the family business.

Estelle poised her pencil over her order pad. "You headed to New York City after you leave?"

"No. Why?"

"Suit. Tie. Shoes polished to a sheen. Not something anyone around here wears, not even to funerals. Ah, here's your company."

Wyatt and his fiancée, Sarah-Jane Early, greeted Estelle, then slid into the booth, never letting go of each other's hands, barely breaking eye contact. What was it about Red Rock that caused so many Fortunes to become love-struck fools? Wyatt made the seventh to succumb in the past two years.

Michael didn't get it. Romantic love was a myth, and marriage nothing more than a practical merger made in the interest of procreation—no matter how it seemed to start. He'd determined long ago that what people called love was really just lust, and that always faded. Respect was the key word. That sustained a relationship. Like his parents' marriage.

"It's nice to see you again," Sarah-Jane said, her long, auburn ponytail swaying when she turned to look at him. Her brown eyes sparkled with friendliness, then went tender when she gazed back at Wyatt.

No one had ever looked at Michael like that. Usually he was the recipient of cool or calculating looks, or just as often, hostile. He didn't hold the important position he did because he went with the flow but because he exulted in riding the more unpredictable rapids. As for personal relationships, casual and short-term didn't result in loving or tender looks, either.

"You've already turned Texan," Michael said, noting Wyatt's jeans and cowboy boots.

"You should try it. Maybe loosen up that corporate stiffness from wearing suits and ties all the time."

Michael took the kidding easily. "I don't wear a suit on the golf course. Or jeans. Not allowed, you know. I understand congratulations are in order," he said, changing the subject. "When's the wedding?"

"In June," Sarah-Jane answered.

"I wouldn't mind eloping," Wyatt said with a put-upon expression. "But she wants her wedding. Women."

Eyes sparkling, she wriggled her nose at him, signaling a private joke between them.

Estelle moseyed over, plucked menus from behind the napkin dispenser and passed them out.

"What would you recommend?" Michael asked her.

She laughed at that. "Well, la-di-dah. I'm some

kinda New York *server,* now. Isn't that how they do that there?"

"I'm sure you're right, but you own the place. Don't you have particular favorites yourself?"

"Sure I do. Tell me, do you like hearty food that'll stick with you 'til dinner or do you go for fruits and grains and mid-afternoon stomach pangs?"

"Fill me up. You choose with what. Surprise me."

"Maybe there's hope for you yet, Suit."

Sarah-Jane laughed at the nickname, then ordered a Cobb salad.

"So I think I've got this figured out," Estelle said to Michael after Wyatt ordered a hamburger. "You're here to try and talk the Fortune boys into going home. You must be one brave man."

Michael realized he'd made a tactical error in letting Wyatt schedule the meeting place. He should've taken care of the arrangements himself, maybe in San Antonio, away from the gossip-filled Red Rock.

Wyatt sat back casually. "Estelle's right, isn't she?" he asked after she'd left. "My father put you up to this little confab. Shane told me you already talked with him."

Back in Atlanta, Michael had drawn a blank with Wyatt's oldest brother, Shane, who was the COO of JMF Financials. He'd left the company but not the city. Although he was the only one of the sons who hadn't moved to Red Rock, Shane was on the same quest as his brothers, to find the woman their father had involved in their business without their knowledge.

"I figure you'll try Asher and Sawyer next," Wyatt

said. "Good luck with that. You won't be changing any-one's minds. You know, Mike, I appreciate your concern, but this really isn't your business…or your call." Wyatt toasted Michael with his glass of water. "I'm never going back. My place is with Sarah-Jane, and Sarah-Jane's place is here in Red Rock."

"How can you not go back? You're a vice president. Your brothers hold top positions, too, and yet you all walked away. I don't understand why you can't ride this out."

"Ride it out? Seriously? My father is giving away half his shares of the company. *Giving* them away. To some unknown woman for an unknown reason. And you're siding with *him* over this?" Wyatt shook his head. "I guess I shouldn't be surprised. You sharks fish in the same waters. How can you—"

Sarah-Jane laid her hand on his, stopping him. Calming him.

Coming from a man Michael had known his entire life, the words stung. "It's your *family* business," Michael said quietly, respecting Sarah-Jane's discomfort and not wanting things to heat up any further.

"But we're not slaves to it," Wyatt said, just as quietly.

"What will you do?"

He looked at Sarah-Jane for a moment. "I'm not a hundred percent sure. I'm working on some things. I just know that Red Rock is home now. My brothers and I have bought property here, a ranch. I don't know what my role is yet. In the end, it may have nothing to do with the ranch." He eyed Sarah-Jane again. "Once I got over my own shock of leaving the company, I realized it was for the best—for me, anyway. I might have been stuck there forever. I'm feeling a freedom I never have before. It feels good."

Estelle set their lunch plates in front of them. "Cobb salad for Miss Sarah-Jane, hamburger for Wyatt and Estelle's famous Reuben for the Suit. Enjoy."

"I love you like a brother, Mike," Wyatt said, picking up a French fry. "The six of you kids and the five of us spent our whole lives like one family, even with our fathers at odds. But you need to stay out of this, unless you want our relationship destroyed as well."

Michael didn't know what he could do to ease the tension, then just when he considered apologizing, Sarah-Jane beckoned someone with a frantic gesture, looking relieved at the interruption. "Felicity! Over here!"

Michael glanced toward the entrance. A woman with shoulder-length blond hair and soft blue eyes walked toward their booth. Her smile lit up the room. Not beautiful, Michael decided, but fresh-faced and, well, adorable. He was sure he'd never used that word to describe a woman before. Or even a kitten. Although she looked kittenish in her fluffy pink sweater and jeans that weren't red, exactly, but a color he couldn't put a name to.

"Sit down," Sarah-Jane said, in a tone more like an order, desperation in her eyes. "Join us."

The slender woman gave Sarah-Jane an amused and curious look, but sat without argument. She took up little space as she slid into the booth next to Michael, but their arms brushed, and he went still. His body felt supercharged, paralyzed. He'd known plenty of women, but he'd never had such a visceral reaction to one, and certainly not one this innocent-looking. What the hell was going on?

She finally made eye contact. Her smile faltered a moment, then, angling toward him, she put out her hand. "Hi. I—I'm Felicity Thomas. Sarah-Jane and I are roommates."

"Michael Fortune." This time he wasn't surprised at the lightning he encountered in her touch, but he still couldn't understand his reaction.

Her brows raised. "Fortune? You're…"

"My first cousin," Wyatt said.

"So, you're Wendy's brother? It's hard to keep all you Fortunes straight. I adore Wendy. She was my first big client."

"For what?"

"My truffles."

"Truffles?" was all he could think to say.

"Wendy had just become the pastry chef at Red. Have you eaten there?" Felicity asked.

Michael nodded.

"She wanted to offer a dessert created with my products."

"Truffles?" he repeated, the only word he'd really picked up clearly.

She cocked her head at him, and he wondered if he could be any more idiotic. What was wrong with him?

"Yes," she said patiently, her smile never fading. "It

turns out that they're a big hit at the local hotels and spas, too. People seem to like them."

"Not to mention a certain competition you just won in Dallas," Sarah-Jane said. "Orders have boomed."

Felicity nodded. "Which is why I'm going to have to make decisions soon."

He shook himself. "About what?"

"About whether or not to grow my business. I've been stretching myself to the limit."

He was fascinated. Entranced. Beguiled. "So, you're a candy maker?"

"My official job title would be confectioner."

She was a confection, all right, all spun sugar and sweetness. He usually preferred his women savory.

"I've been hogging the conversation, haven't I?" she asked with an apologetic smile and a friendly touch on his arm.

Even through his suit jacket he felt the heat.

"How about you?" she asked. "Which Fortune captain of industry are you?"

He'd never seen eyes so blue or hair so shiny, and it took him a moment to realize she was expecting an answer. "I'm chief operating officer of FortuneSouth Enterprises in Atlanta. It's a telecommunications company my father built."

"That's different from Wyatt's. Or the one he used to work for anyway."

Which remains to be seen, Michael thought. He wasn't done with Wyatt yet. "Wyatt's father and mine are brothers. Each built their own business. Until now, they've both been family-run."

"We don't really need to talk business, do we?" Sarah-Jane asked, her voice strained. "Felicity, would you like some of my salad? I can't eat it all."

"Or order what you'd like," Michael said, gesturing to Estelle. *Stay awhile. Talk to me some more.*

"I've had lunch, thanks. I was making a delivery and saw you—um, Sarah-Jane and Wyatt—through the window. I need to get back to the shop. Thirteen days and counting, you know."

"Until?"

She leaned toward him, her hair catching against his suit jacket, and whispered loudly, "The apocalypse."

She smelled of chocolate and mint. He wanted to press his lips against her skin and taste it. "Pardon?" he said, clenching his fists.

She looked around stealthily. "Valentine's Day. The total devastation of my painstakingly created candy supply."

If Sarah-Jane sparkled, Felicity was an entire fireworks display.

"I'll come with you and help," Sarah-Jane said, hopping up and grabbing Felicity's hand. "I've got about a half hour before I need to get back to work. You don't mind, do you?" she asked Wyatt.

"I—"

But the women were already gone. Sarah-Jane hadn't kissed Wyatt goodbye, which said a lot to Michael. "In a bit of a hurry to get her friend out of here, wasn't she?"

"Stay away from Felicity," Wyatt said, not holding back for a second. "She's not like the sophisticated women you're used to."

Much like his father, Michael wasn't used to hearing the word *no.* Telling him he couldn't have Felicity was tantamount to waving a red flag in front of a bull. "Just like with you and Sarah-Jane, I believe."

"Felicity is *not* fling material. If you want a date while you're here, I'm sure there are plenty of women who would be thrilled to keep you company."

"I won't sleep with her." He had no idea where those words came from. They'd just spilled out.

Wyatt laughed. "Right. Sure."

"She'll just be a pleasant distraction. I'm not staying long."

"Not even if she begs," Wyatt said, pointing a finger.

"Is that a possibility?"

"Let me offer you a few words of advice, because you're new around here. If you break Felicity's heart, everyone will hear about it. She's the marrying kind, Mike. Even if the unthinkable happens and you fall for each other, you won't leave Atlanta, and she won't leave Red Rock. She's small-town and likes it."

"That's not the point. I'm not talking marriage here." Although, at age thirty-six, he should be starting to think about it. He just hadn't met the right woman, the perfect corporate wife, like his mother—sedate, social and proper.

That didn't mean he couldn't act on his attraction to a woman who wasn't marriage material. That was all he'd ever done. Except this woman *was* different. He needed to acknowledge that, if only to himself.

"Stay away from her, Mike," Wyatt repeated more coldly. "If you break Felicity's heart, Sarah-Jane will somehow hold me responsible. That wouldn't be something I can fix. And it would leave a bad taste in people's mouths about all of us Fortunes."

"I already said I wouldn't sleep with her." But damned if he would let his cousin tell him what he could or couldn't do.

He paid the bill, then they walked out together, saying a terse goodbye before going in opposite directions, tension lingering between them. Michael pulled his phone out of his pocket and called his uncle, not telling the older man how badly he'd screwed up, only that it would take more time than he'd expected. He'd started his campaign with Wyatt because he'd always been the most flexible. His brothers would be even more of a challenge.

"Don't give up," Uncle James said.

"Not my style." Not in business. Not in life. His father had taught him that, too. "I'll try Asher next."

"Good. Keep in touch."

"Will do." Michael ended the call, then immediately placed another to his assistant in Atlanta, then he made his way back to his hotel to work out a game plan. He had two causes to fulfill, and right now, both seemed way out of reach.

"You can relax your death grip on my arm now," Felicity muttered to Sarah-Jane as they made the short walk to the coffee house where Felicity rented space for her wares. "Maybe you should just use this half hour to go to the park, where you usually go for lunch. You need to calm down."

Sarah-Jane let go. "Sorry."

"Why did you pull me away? I was having a good time."

"Too good."

"What's that supposed to mean?"

"I mean Cupid's bow shot an arrow directly into your heart the minute you laid eyes on Michael Fortune. I saw it. Everyone saw it."

That gave Felicity pause. "Totally your imagination."

"I've never seen you flirt like that. You touched him, even leaned against him. That's not you. Not that quickly."

"It wasn't as bad as all that…was it?"

Sarah-Jane gave her a look.

Felicity sighed. "When you told me about the five Fortune men lined up at the bar on New Year's Eve and you said each one was handsomer than the next, I figured you were exaggerating. You were certainly right about four of them, and now the fifth has arrived. And he's like Prince Charming out of central casting."

"He's a hard-hearted corporate raider. Wyatt's told me all about him. He's ruthless."

"When it's not business, though, but personal? Did you talk about that?"

Sarah-Jane frowned. "No."

"He didn't exactly flirt back, you know." Felicity knew he'd been paying attention, but he hadn't turned on the charm. In fact, he'd said precious little. She'd dominated the conversation, as usual talking too much when she was nervous. Her first sight of him had definitely made her nervous. Or something.

Felicity fretted about it as they went through the door of Break Time, the tea and coffee shop where she leased space for her candy business, True Confections. Within the shop itself, her station was small, but it was the prep area in the back she'd needed so badly, especially at big holidays. For her, Valentine's Day started weeks before the actual day.

The holiday was close enough now that she'd brought in the big gun, her aunt Liz, who was her silent partner. Wearing a walking cast after breaking a bone in her foot, Liz sat behind the display case, her chin-length, curly red hair a beacon of comfort, confidence and lifetime affection. She looked up and smiled.

Sarah-Jane strode right past her and into the kitchen behind, muttering, "Your niece is in lust," before disappearing through the swinging door.

"Again?" Liz asked, grinning.

Sarah-Jane peeked out of the door. "She wouldn't be able to lead this one around by the collar."

Liz's brows arched high. "Do tell."

"She's exaggerating as usual." Felicity grabbed an apron, a pretty aqua-colored fabric with True Confections imprinted in gold lettering on the ties, just like her signature boxes and ribbons. She washed her hands, keeping her back to her aunt. "I just met him. We spent all of two minutes together."

"And sparks were flying so fast and furious I had to duck or get burned," Sarah-Jane called out from the back room.

"Were there sparks from him, too?" Liz asked Felicity.

"I don't know. I couldn't tell." She checked the inventory in the glass case, knowing full well her aunt would've already taken care of it.

"Is this different from any other time?" Liz asked softly.

Felicity didn't answer, trying to decide. It was more physical than any other, she thought. She liked the way he looked and wanted to be close to him. She was drawn in by his dark hair and eyes, opposite of her own. And he looked like he worked out. In fact, she'd wanted to lean against his hard body. He seemed tall enough that she could fit comfortably under his chin. His arms would be strong and comforting…and arousing.

"Earth to Felicity," Liz said, snapping her fingers in front of Felicity's eyes.

She heaved a huge sigh. "This is all just crazy. He lives in Atlanta. He's some big corporate guy with a ton of money and status. What would he see in a small-town girl like me? Plus, he won't be around for long."

And for some reason, that thought more than any other made her feel as though her bubble had burst, even though it had barely had time to form a transparent shell around her.

Sarah-Jane joined them behind the counter. She slid her arm around Felicity's waist. "You are gorgeous and sweet and can date any man you want. Just not *him,* okay?"

"Need I remind you of my many failed relationships?" At twenty-four, she'd had her share of dates, but many of the men lost interest when they found out she was a virgin and wouldn't put out on the third date. She'd been waiting a long time to find The One.

"You deserve to be courted," Sarah-Jane said, "not managed like a business deal, and that's how he would operate. Wyatt told me Michael has no soft center. That kind of man doesn't have a romantic bone in his body."

"Michael?" Liz asked.

"Fortune. Wyatt's cousin."

Liz shook her head, her curls bouncing. "Pretty soon we're going to have to rename our town after that family. They've been swarming like locusts. How old is this Michael Fortune?"

"Thirty-six," Sarah-Jane answered. "He's the oldest of his and Wyatt's siblings. Apparently he's been bossing everyone around all his life."

"Not necessarily a bad quality," Liz said thoughtfully. "Alpha males make interesting companions."

The bell over the front door jangled and in came CarolAnn the florist carrying a vase with a bouquet of red roses. She headed straight to the candy counter.

Felicity sighed. Wyatt was so romantic, frequently sending or bringing Sarah-Jane little gifts. She was a lucky girl. He always let her know how much she meant to him.

But CarolAnn set them on the counter, then winked at Felicity, not Sarah-Jane. "Someone's been a very good girl. Or maybe not." She grinned, then left.

Dazed, Felicity plucked the card from its holder, burying her face in the blooms as she did. The heady scent spiraled inside her.

It was a pleasure to meet you. Michael Fortune.

"Lemme see. Lemme see," Sarah-Jane said, reaching for the card.

Felicity didn't want to share it. While they weren't romantic words, they were private. And thrilling to her.

The shop phone rang. Felicity grabbed it, needing to do something normal. "True Confections," she said in her upbeat business voice.

"Are the flowers to your liking?"

Felicity's heart registered one big thump, then didn't let up. Her throat almost closed. "Very much so. Thank you." She would've said more, like how beautiful they were and how fragrant, but she couldn't say another word.

"Have dinner with me tonight," he said.

She nodded, then, flustered, realized he couldn't see her. "Okay."

"I'll pick you up at six at your apartment. I know where you live."

"Jeans or dress?" she managed to ask, wanting to look right for the occasion.

"Dress." Although he'd said only one word, his tone of voice turned it into a sentence. *Wear something feminine,* she heard. *Sexy.*

She ran a quick mental inventory of her closet. Yes, she had the perfect outfit.

"See you soon," he said, ending the conversation before she even said goodbye.

"Stars in her eyes," Sarah-Jane said. "Lost in space. Definitely Michael Fortune on the phone."

"We're having dinner tonight," Felicity said, tucking the florist's card into her pocket and her anticipation into her heart. Love at first sight. They'd just been words before, an unproven possibility.

"You'll wear the red dress I gave you for Christmas," Liz said. "And the silver high heels."

"Yes." Felicity looked at Sarah-Jane. "I helped you with a makeover when you were dating Wyatt."

"My Swarovski evening bag would look perfect." Sarah-Jane sighed.

"Cinderella going to the ball," Felicity said, scared but smiling.

"Be home before midnight," her roommate said, shaking a finger, then turning away. "I'm sorry there's no time to help after all. Work calls."

After she left, Liz hugged Felicity. "Even if it's only for one night, sweetheart, enjoy it."

"How could it be more than that anyway? Talk about the ultimate nothing-in-common, opposites-attract couple."

"One never knows. Life is full of mysteries, and aren't we glad of it."

Felicity stepped away, smiling. "I need to try to remember not to talk so much."

"You need to be yourself, and that's all. He spent a few minutes with you and was smitten. That should tell you enough."

"I think he's a man who makes up his mind fast and goes after what he wants. And then walks away easily when he's done," she added, trying to prepare herself for the inevitable.

"What matters most, Felicity, is how you feel. That's

the only thing you can control. Not his feelings, only yours. Don't have regrets."

A huge bright light flashed in Felicity's head. Liz was right. Of course she was right.

Felicity would just be herself. Enjoy herself.

And maybe she'd be the one this time to say, "It's been fun, but I don't see this going any further."

Except somehow she couldn't imagine that happening.

Chapter Two

Felicity twirled in front of the mirror, appraising the fit of her sleeveless sheath. In deference to the temperature, she carried an ethereal-looking shawl with silver sparkles. Her necklace was a simple diamond drop that had been a gift to her aunt from an admirer many years ago, along with matching earrings.

She felt sophisticated. She'd even curled her hair a little instead of leaving it straight, her usual style. She stared into the mirror. Somewhere in there was the Felicity she knew. So much for being herself.

She went downstairs to await Michael's arrival, not wanting to make a grand entrance after he got there, afraid she would stumble. What an impression that would make.

"He's definitely not going to be discouraged," Sarah-

Jane said, her arms crossed. "You cleaned up well. Too well, I'd say."

The doorbell rang. Precisely six o'clock. Sarah-Jane started to go to the door, but Felicity needed to *do* something, to move her feet before she rooted in place, nerves almost nailing her to the floor. "I'll get it," she told her friend.

He didn't look much different from before. He wore a suit then and now. White shirt, dark tie. But his face, his handsome face, looked even more intense, more sharply angled and…fascinating.

"Hi," he said, when she'd been sure he would say "good evening" or something much more formal.

She found she could smile after all. "Hi. Would you like to come in?"

"We have six-thirty reservations." He glanced into the room. She saw his gaze land on the vase of flowers she'd brought home from the shop, then move on to Sarah-Jane, who gave a reluctant wave.

Felicity picked up her evening bag and shawl, which Michael took from her, then draped over her shoulders, his fingers resting there for a beat or two, long enough to steal her breath.

"You kids have fun," Sarah-Jane said.

"What will you and Wyatt be doing?" Michael asked.

"Taking advantage of having the place to ourselves."

Felicity caught her roommate giving Michael an I'm-watching-you look. "She's overprotective," Felicity said as she and Michael headed across the apartment court-yard with its lighted pool. "She's three years older than me and maternal."

"It's good having someone watching your back," he said, setting a hand low on her spine. "Have you been friends long?"

They'd reached the complex's parking lot. She picked out his car right away. In a town where pickup trucks ruled, his sleek black sports car stood out.

"My dad's sister, Liz, moved to Red Rock a long time ago. I spent summers here all through high school and two years of college, learning the candy business from her. I moved here permanently four years ago when I was twenty. Sarah-Jane and I met a year later at the coffee shop right after she'd moved here. The friendship was instantaneous."

She slipped into the fine leather seat as he held the car door for her, then watched him walk around the vehicle, his movements fluid. He got inside, slid the key in but didn't start the engine. Uncharacteristically, she waited for him to speak.

He caught and held her gaze. "Thank you for accepting my invitation."

"My pleasure."

He smiled, something he hadn't done a whole lot of since she'd met him. "I assure you, the pleasure is mine."

"Looks like we have a mutual pleasure society," she said before realizing how it sounded. "I mean—"

"I understood what you meant. And I concur."

He started the car and pulled out of the parking lot. The evening was crisp and clear. "What do you think of Red Rock?" she asked.

"It's…quaint."

"But no place you'd want to live."

"I like Atlanta," he answered evasively. "What drew you to it?"

"I came from Dallas, so I've done the big-city thing. It's not that I didn't love my city, but from the first time I came to visit my aunt, I felt at home."

"Is your family still in Dallas?"

"Yes. I don't see them budging. My parents have been happily married for thirty-two years. I have two older sisters, Megan and Lila, and they're both also happily married and living in Dallas." She realized she was talking too much and too fast. "But enough about me. Sarah-Jane tells me you have five siblings. That must've been something, that many kids in one house."

"Never a dull moment. Are you and my sister friends?"

The sudden change of subject signaled to Felicity that he was done talking about himself. "Wendy and I don't hang out together much, but we're friendly. She has a lot of…energy."

"Since the day she came home from the hospital." He glanced her way. "Have you eaten at Vines and Roses?"

"Is that where we're going?" She shook her head. It was a special-occasion restaurant. "No, I haven't, but I've heard about it."

Gnarly grapevines hung in dark silhouette as Michael and Felicity drove up to the entrance. Leaves wouldn't appear until next month, but Felicity also enjoyed the starkness of the barren vines.

"When I was a kid," she said, "I took part in a grape stomping event at a small county fair. My feet were purple for a week. My mom was going to bleach them, but I wouldn't let her. I wore sandals all week, I was so proud."

"A budding Lucille Ball," he said, grinning.

"That was the impetus for the event. We were supposed to dress up like her in that episode. My mom made me a costume that looked just like hers, too. I didn't squeeze out the most juice, but I won the blue ribbon for my costume. Oh! Isn't the restaurant wonderful!"

The restaurant itself was understated and elegant, their table situated in a heated patio that was surrounded by a grove of trees. Felicity looked around, dazzled by it all and openly pleased. When she looked at Michael, he smiled. She liked his smile.

"I take it the place meets your approval," he said.

"It's beautiful."

"I didn't order your main course, but I did arrange for appetizers and champagne," he said as a waiter approached. "I hope that's all right with you."

A flurry of activity ensued, a well-practiced dance of host, server and other staff, quiet and efficient. Champagne was poured, and a plate with four parmesan-crusted colossal shrimp was set before them, along with a spicy marinara dipping sauce.

Michael lifted his champagne flute to her, waiting for her to touch glasses. "To the lovely confectioner," he said, taking a sip, watching her over the rim. He appreciated her enthusiasm, the way she didn't attempt to hide her excitement at the plans he'd made. He'd been dating too many jaded women, he decided. Not that he wasn't jaded himself. He was. And it wasn't a matter of having forgotten what it was like to be with someone who was so comfortable in her own skin. He hadn't forgotten, because he'd rarely been in that position, having generally dated women who were the opposite of Felicity in personality.

It made him relax with her in a way he couldn't remember relaxing before.

They talked and ate and drank. She ordered chicken-fried Cornish game hen served with a green chili cornbread stuffing and topped with a Southwestern cream sauce. He ordered beef tenderloin with a creamy garlic and mushroom sauce, with garlic mashed potatoes and perfectly roasted asparagus. They finished by sharing a slice of German chocolate cake.

"I wonder what they would call me if I was paying the bill," she commented as she forked up the crumbs.

"What do you mean?"

"You have been called Mr. Fortune at least twenty times tonight. I am referred to as 'the lady.' Do you suppose if the bill were coming to me, I would be Ms. Thomas and you would be 'the gentleman'?"

He hadn't noticed. Was that chauvinistic? "I guess that bothered you."

"Your reputation—or at least your name—precedes you. I imagine you're used to being catered to."

"Feel free to pay the bill yourself and see what happens."

She patted her hips as if looking for something. "Oh, darn. I left my wallet at home."

"Then *the lady* will have to suffer the consequences."

If she'd had any food left on her plate, she might have tossed it at him, Michael thought. He liked her sass, liked that she was openly happy about being with him.

They spent two hours being taken care of. Their conversation wasn't extraordinary in content, but the usual getting-to-know-you back and forth, and yet attraction crackled and sparked tangibly between them.

"It's still early," he said as they started the drive back to Red Rock. "Would you like to take a longer route home? There's enough moonlight to see the sights."

She turned to him and smiled sweetly. "I would." She laid her hand on his for a moment as it curled over the gearshift. When she pulled it back, he reached over and wrapped his fingers around hers, resting his hand on her thigh. He felt those muscles tighten, but he didn't let go.

Counting on the car's GPS unit to get him back to Red Rock eventually, Michael just drove. Occasionally she would comment on where they were, but mostly they sat in companionable silence as they drove past farmland and ranchland, big, spacious properties with a house set back among trees, generally, and barns, corrals and other outbuildings mostly hidden, sheltered from wind.

At one point she said, "This is where your cousin Victoria lives with her husband, Garrett. You should stop by and see them, if you have time. There's lots going on there. A new house, new buildings for their animal rescue sanctuary. Unless you're leaving right away?"

He squeezed her hand. "I'm not."

"How long are you staying?" Her voice seemed tight.

"It depends on the results of a couple of meetings," he said, knowing he would be dragging out his visit as long as possible, but not knowing how long he could effectively work from Red Rock. "I can't stay away too long, especially now. We're in the process of buying out a smaller company."

"This is one of the busiest times of the year for me, too."

"You sound pretty calm to me."

"Lists. Calendars. Schedules. I live, breathe, eat and sleep by them."

He wouldn't have pegged her as an organizer. Obviously there were hidden talents beneath the surface of her bubbly personality.

"Sarah-Jane mentioned you won some kind of competition?"

"Last month in Dallas. It was a truffle competition. I took first and third place."

"Among how many entries?"

"You *are* a businessman," she said, grinning. "There were more than two contestants."

"Three?"

"Thirty-two."

That *was* impressive. "Congratulations."

"Thanks. I was pretty happy. I was given two plaques to put in my shop, and the *Dallas Morning News* ran an article, as well as the *San Antonio Express-News*. And our local paper, of course."

"I'll bet your internet sales increased, and that's why you said before that you have decisions to make about growing your business."

"It's not just individual consumers. The newspaper articles talked about my hotel and spa business, too, which I've been slowly growing—pillow mints, things like that. I've been comfortable with my little shop, and yet..."

He gave her a quick glance. There was a wistfulness in her voice. "And yet?"

"I want to accomplish more, Michael."

It was the first time she'd said his name, and he was surprised by how his gut clenched. It seemed...intimate somehow.

"How many hours do you put in? Could you manage more?"

"I'm open from eleven in the morning until five-thirty in the evening, Tuesday through Saturday, but that's just the retail aspect. I also have to make the products."

"You're happy with the work?"

"Oh, yes. And I'm good at it. I keep experimenting and learning. Every so often I have taste-testing days for the public. Liz thought I was crazy for giving away so much, but I found it led to more sales. Many more."

They'd reached downtown Red Rock. He'd ignored the clock, letting their conversation dictate how long they would take. But he saw it was eleven and knew she had to get up early. He pulled into her parking lot, then didn't make a move to exit the car. "What's your favorite candy that you make?"

"Triple chocolate truffle. It's sinful. I brought you a sample." She opened her evening bag. Tucked inside was a small box tied with ribbon. "Want to take a bite of sin?" she asked.

Her tone was flirtatious, not seductive, yet he wanted to take her to his hotel room and really get sinful.

She didn't wait for his answer, but pulled off the ribbon and opened the box. One truffle nested there. She brought it up to his mouth. He took a bite—

She might call it sin, but to him it was heaven. She offered the remaining half. He was tempted, but instead took it from her and held it to her mouth. The feel of her lips touching his fingers aroused him—and frustrated him, too.

He wasn't sure what to do about her yet, other than enjoying her company. He'd promised Wyatt he wouldn't sleep with her, *even if she begged....*

"That was amazing," he said. "The best I've ever had."

She ran her tongue over a spot of chocolate at the corner of her mouth, catching it. "I'm glad you enjoyed it. I make the same recipe but with cayenne pepper in it. Do you like spicy?"

"I'm particularly fond of spicy," he said. He eyed her. She looked right back. "Especially where the flavor doesn't hit you at first bite. But when it does, it's powerful, and then it lingers."

Michael wrapped his hand around hers again, emphasizing the point he was making.

"That's how I would describe that particular truffle," she said, rubbing her thumb along his hand.

"Which one of your candies describes *you?*"

A smile tugged slowly at her mouth. "I'm a candy cane."

"Only available at Christmas?"

She threw her head back, laughing. "What you see is what you get. No change of flavor halfway. Consistent."

She was obviously too sweet for the likes of him. And yet…he was enjoying her company more than anyone's he had for a very long time. It was rare to come across someone who wasn't cynical. Or bored. Boredom was pervasive in his circle, or at least the appearance of boredom, as if showing excitement about anything made you less than cool. He was guilty of it himself.

He decided to do things differently this time. No kiss goodnight. Well, no *big* kiss, just something to tease her, make her hungry for more. He hoped to give more—and take more—soon.

He held her hand as he walked her to her door a few seconds later.

"Wyatt must've left," she said. "His car isn't here."

"They're not sleeping together?" That seemed impossible to him.

"Not every night. Sarah-Jane probably had work to do."

At her door, Felicity ran her hands down his lapels, then let them drop away and stared at his chest, worried she was being too bold. She felt him finger her hair, tucking a strand behind her ear. "Would you like to come in?" she asked.

"It's late, and we both have to be up early. I had a good time, Felicity."

"Me, too." *Kiss me, please kiss me.*

He brushed his lips briefly against hers. "Good night."

She'd just begun to enjoy the kiss when he ended it. "Um, thank you for everything, Michael," she said, trying to find her equilibrium. She managed to unlock the door and go inside, knowing he was waiting until she did so, then she rushed to the window and watched him fade into the night. She ran upstairs, knocked on Sarah-Jane's door, then went in without waiting to be invited. She jumped on the bed. Sarah-Jane sat straight up, holding her arms out protectively.

"What the— Felicity! What's going on? Are you all right? I knew you shouldn't have gone out with him. What did he do?"

Felicity took a deep, settling breath. "Sarah-Jane, I have met the man I'm going to marry."

"Yeah? A waiter at the restaurant? The valet? The chef?"

Felicity laughed. "You know who. He's nothing like you said, nothing like Wyatt told you. He's a good listener and a true gentleman."

Sarah-Jane shook her head. "I was afraid of this."

"Be happy for me." Felicity climbed off the bed, her mood shifting from the high she'd been on. "Don't I have the same right as you to find the love of my life?"

"Wyatt wasn't a player nor was he unyielding," Sarah-Jane said quietly. "But you made your point. Of course you have the same right. It's just…"

"He lives in Atlanta and I live in Red Rock," Felicity said, finishing the sentence. "He's a man of the world, and I'm a woman of an everybody-knows-your-business town. I'm a virgin. I would guess he's not." She smiled at her friend. "Stranger things have happened."

Sarah-Jane hugged her. "I'm sorry. You're a big girl. You get to make your own decisions."

"Thank you. If it goes south, I won't run to you for comfort."

"You will and you should. That's what best friends are for—truth and comfort."

They hugged once more, then Felicity headed for the door.

"Did he ask you for a second date?" Sarah-Jane asked.

"No." She uttered the word lightly, casually, even though she worried that he hadn't.

Sarah-Jane didn't say a word. She didn't have to. But Felicity wasn't going to let anything ruin this perfect evening.

A few minutes later, she slipped into bed. How was she supposed to sleep now? She replayed the evening, especially all the times he touched her. Then at the end of the evening, the lightest of kisses, leaving her wanting more—undoubtedly his intention. Although she would've liked for him to have lost control, gotten carried away and kissed her senseless.

Why, oh, why had he come to town now when she had so much to do, so little time to spend with him? It didn't sound as if he intended to move to Red Rock like so many of his siblings and cousins, although having family here gave him plenty of reasons to visit, so this probably wouldn't be their only chance to get to know each other.

Felicity blew out a breath. Why was she even thinking that far ahead? He probably just wanted someone to pass the time with, and she was handy—and adoring. He had to have seen the infatuation in her eyes every time she looked at him. Who wouldn't be flattered by that kind of attention?

She shoved her hair back from her face. He was so completely different from any man she'd dated. He knew himself, not only knew what he wanted to do the rest of his life but was already doing it. Successfully. He was confident, too, which appealed to her a lot. He would want a strong woman, one who matched him in confidence.

Saying no to him seemed impossible.

But first he had to give her a chance to say yes.

Chapter Three

Michael stepped into Estelle's the next morning to meet his cousin Asher, who waved from the first booth. The last time they'd been together was for Michael's sister Emily's wedding on New Year's Eve. He had to admit that Asher looked relaxed, just as Wyatt had. Also like Wyatt, Asher had dirty-blond hair and blue eyes, the family resemblance strong, and those eyes both welcomed and studied Michael.

Asher stood and pounded a hug on Michael's back. He hadn't realized how much he'd been missing his cousins and siblings since they'd abandoned Atlanta. "Good to see you, Ash." He looked around, recalling his first visit here yesterday. "Great choice."

"All the locals come here. Basic, down-home food, and this beautiful lady, too," he said, grinning as Estelle sauntered over carrying a coffeepot.

"We've met," Michael said, flipping over his mug.

"Welcome back, Suit. You know, if you stay a day or two longer, you'd better get yourself some Wranglers. People won't trust you." She refilled Asher's mug, then turned away. "I'll be back for your order in a coupla shakes."

"The whole town seems to be filled with characters like that," Michael said, grabbing a menu from behind the napkin dispenser.

"They're good, decent people, and yes, some of them are characters."

"No need to get defensive, Ash. I didn't mean anything by the observation. I like Estelle. She says what's on her mind."

"I just want to get this over with." Asher shoved his menu back in place. "I know why you wanted to have breakfast together."

"Why's that?"

"To convince me to go back to JMF."

Michael leaned back. "I'm beginning to understand that none of you plan to do that, but does it mean you have to leave Atlanta altogether? You have parents who want to spend time with their four-year-old grandson. And he's missing out on having a relationship with them."

"Jace is thriving here. It was the best decision I've made. And I'm healing, too. Recovery from a divorce like mine doesn't come easily. Anyway, the situation is complicated. Jace still expects his mother to walk back through the door."

"Do you expect that, too?"

"I haven't heard from Lynn in six months. She said she needed a clean break, including from her son. How do I explain that to a vulnerable little boy?"

Michael shook his head, not knowing the answer, either. "I will never understand how Lynn could turn her back on her family that way. Once you've made the commitment, it should stick, no matter what."

"Spoken like a man who hasn't committed yet—or survived the aftermath. Some marriages really can't be saved. And Lynn wasn't entirely to blame."

"Seems to me it's the institution of marriage that's to blame. It sets up unrealistic expectations that no one can fulfill." After the cynicism-free evening he'd had with Felicity, Michael didn't like the glaring return of it now.

"There are good marriages out there, Mike. We've all seen them."

Estelle came back, order pad in hand.

"What would you recommend?" Michael asked her, hiding a smile.

She laughed at that. "Here we go again."

"The Reuben was the best I've ever had. I assume you have breakfast favorites that rank as high as that."

"Sure I do."

"Then you choose. You did great before."

"I'll surprise you, then, Suit."

"It's fun watching you reel someone in," Asher said after Estelle left.

Michael hadn't thought he'd been doing that. Manipulation was one tool of many in business, but he hadn't manipulated her, not on purpose. And truthfully, it threw him for a loop that Asher thought he had.

"So, how was your date with Felicity?" Asher asked.

Michael wasn't really surprised that Asher knew. "Wyatt's not too happy about that."

"Yeah? I can't say that's a shocker, but I didn't hear about it from my brother."

"Who, then?"

He pointed toward Estelle.

"Which means the whole town knows?" Michael asked, not pleased.

"Probably not the *whole* town. Though everyone around here likes Felicity."

"What's not to like?" Michael pictured her. "She's attractive and good company."

"And I'll remind you that she's roommates with someone who's about to become part of our family, my future sister-in-law. Let's not sully the Fortune name so quickly in Red Rock by breaking her best friend's heart."

Michael's jaw clenched. "You have a pretty low opinion of me."

"I have an honest opinion of you, Mike, based on a lifetime of knowing you. You always get what you want."

"What I *work* for."

Asher nodded. "But you're thirty-six now and well past the age when you should feel the need for conquests."

"You've become quite a philosopher since moving here."

"I'm a single dad, trying to keep my son from hurting any more than he already is. I've learned to be more careful with people's feelings. I ask that you tread cautiously with Felicity. I've met her on only a few occasions, but as you've learned, everyone around here talks. I know she's a treasure for someone. *Someday*."

The implied warning settled the debate Michael had been waging with himself. Torn between asking Felicity out again or leaving her alone became a simple decision now.

"I'd like to see you again."

Felicity held the phone a little closer to her ear as she went through the door to the prep room and stepped into the quieter space. She wasn't open for business yet, but people were milling about in the coffee shop.

"I'd like that, too, Michael," she said. "The problem is when."

"What's your schedule for the day?"

"My aunt is coming in to run the shop for a few hours because I need to go to San Antonio and pick up some supplies." She had a master list for the next twelve days. If she didn't stick to it, she wouldn't be able to fill her orders, and that would be disastrous.

"What time are you leaving?" he asked.

"In an hour."

"May I go with you?"

"To the warehouse?"

"Are there rules against it?"

"No, but I doubt it will be interesting to you."

"I find everything about you interesting, Felicity."

"Oh. Well." She fumbled for words. Good grief, what

a thing to say to her. "Okay, then. We'll need to take my pickup because I'll have cases to bring back."

"You drive a pickup?"

"It's practical."

"Is it pink?"

She grinned. "What? Macho man doesn't want to be seen in a pink truck? Oh, don't worry. It's not pink."

"Good."

"It's a stick shift." She was having so much fun listening to his hesitations and silences. She'd give anything to see his expression.

"That's a skill in my repertoire." He sounded slightly offended that she would question his masculinity in that way.

"Then you're on."

"I'll see you soon." He hung up before she even got to say goodbye.

Felicity went back to dipping her mint patties in dark chocolate. Some candies she could make ahead, like the batch of salted caramels she'd made earlier. Others, like her specialty truffles, needed to wait until the last few days before Valentine's Day.

Her hands ached. Caramels needed to be wrapped right away or they would lose their square shape. She'd twisted a few hundred caramels in papers, then formed mint patties by hand, liking the free-form shapes. She'd planned her trip to San Antonio this morning purposefully, knowing her hands would need a break before getting back to work this afternoon.

Felicity kept an eye on the viewing window between the kitchen and front room. Michael hadn't said exactly when he would arrive, only "soon." She saw Liz come in and head to the coffee counter. She must have called ahead because a tall cup awaited her.

"Details," Liz said as she came into the prep room. "I want all the details."

"Dinner at Vines and Roses," Felicity replied with a smile, dipping a patty into the chocolate without looking, she'd done it so many times. "Champagne, shrimp, Cornish game hen, German chocolate cake, long drive through the country, a tender kiss on my doorstep."

"You hate shrimp."

"I ate only one. It's not as if I'm allergic, you know, and he'd thoughtfully ordered ahead. I'm sure it seemed generous of me to let him have the other three." She fluttered her eyelashes.

Liz grabbed Felicity, laughing. "You're usually so direct."

"I get that from you." She shrugged. "I didn't want to hurt his feelings."

"Is there a second date?"

"He's going to the Sweets Market with me."

"Is he meeting you here?"

Felicity set the last patty on a parchment-covered tray and carried it to the cooler. "Anytime now. He's even going to drive my truck."

"Has he seen it?"

"No."

"This ought to be interesting." She looked out the viewing window. "And that has to be Michael Fortune."

Felicity's pulse raced, spreading warmth through her veins. He'd left off his tie, his concession to going casual, she guessed. The open collar of his white shirt revealed a vee of skin she wanted to press her lips to. "Yes, that's Michael," she said, brushing her hands down her apron.

"I can see why you fell. He reminds me of someone I knew long ago. Same air of confidence. Same perfect posture."

"The man you moved to Red Rock for? The love of your life?"

"Years and regrets ago. I didn't move here *for* him, but because of him. We'll talk about that another time. For now, all I can say is hubba-hubba, Mr. Michael Fortune. He does seem like a man who people don't often say no to."

He spotted them through the window and came directly back, which was a good thing, Felicity decided. She'd been rooted in place just watching him. It hadn't occurred to her to go out to greet him. She just wanted to stand there and soak him up.

"Good morning," he said.

Felicity moved in for a quick hug, then realized her hands were covered in chocolate. "Liz, I'd like you to meet Michael Fortune. Michael, this is my aunt, Liz Thomas."

As they exchanged a few pleasantries, Felicity realized the coffee shop had gotten noisy enough to hear from the prep room, and customers were moving toward the front window to stare outside. "I wonder what's going on?" she said, curious at the odd behavior.

"Are you ready?" Michael asked.

"Um, yes." She untied her apron, then hung it on a

hook. She pulled her purse and clipboard holding her supply list from a cabinet. "Don't worry about doing anything back here, Liz. Just rest your foot. We won't be too long."

"Maybe a little longer than you had planned," Michael said, urging her forward with a hand at her lower back. "If you don't mind, Liz."

"I'm fine. She's the one with the rigid schedule. If you can change her timeline a little, more power to you."

"I like a challenge."

"I'll bet you do," Liz said, right behind them as they left the kitchen.

Felicity paid no attention to their conversation. Something was happening outside the shop. "What's going on?" she asked the crowd in general.

Every person in the room turned and grinned at her. Michael continued to guide her to the front door. Then she saw it—a big, black limo was parked in front of the store, three cars back from her truck.

"Yours, I assume," she said as they escaped the curious eyes following their every move.

"For a few hours. Meet Jackson," Michael said as the chauffeur opened the door for them.

"I know Jack. Didn't know you were really Jackson. Or that you owned a limo. I only know you love salted caramels."

He touched the brim of his hat, not a chauffeur's cap, which really would've looked ridiculous on him, but a pristine white cowboy hat. "How're you, Miss Felicity?"

"Feeling pretty taken aback at the moment." She

glanced at Michael, who had mastered the art of no reaction.

A limo. She'd ridden in one for her senior prom, sharing it with three other couples, but that had been a tradition.

This was an extravagance. It made her feel distinctly uncomfortable in front of all the townspeople following her every move and expression, but it would make her feel positively ridiculous at the Sweets Market.

She put a hand on Michael's arm and moved him out of Jack's hearing. "I appreciate the gesture, Michael, I really do. But we're taking my truck."

"Why? The limo's large enough to haul your supplies, isn't it?"

"That's not the point." She could feel thirty-plus pairs of eyes zeroed in on her. She tried to keep her expression neutral because of it. "This is a business trip. I need my truck."

"But—"

"I would understand if you decide not to go with me."

His silence lasted a beat or two. "I thought it would give us more time to get to know each other."

"Maybe if you'd asked me first." Maybe, but doubtful. "I don't need those kinds of luxuries, Michael."

He was obviously a good poker player because his face never betrayed his feelings. He just stepped around her and spoke with Jack, who pulled a cooler out of the car, passed it to Michael, then took off.

As Felicity walked to her pretty aqua pickup with its True Confections emblazoned on the doors in gold, she spotted Liz giving her a thumbs-up through the window. *"Be yourself."* Felicity could hear the unspoken words from her strong, independent aunt echo through her mind.

At the truck, Michael put out his hand. She dropped her car keys into his palm. He hefted the cooler. "I brought lunch for the trip back. If that was too presumptuous, I could give it to those teenagers gawking at us."

She liked the barely restrained sarcasm. "What did you bring?" she asked sweetly.

He smiled finally. "Estelle put it together. I haven't even looked."

"Oh, good. That means no caviar or sushi."

They got into the truck and took off. She was glad to leave the prying eyes behind, especially because most people knew she didn't usually wear a lacy blouse and swirly skirt to work, like she had on today. She'd hoped to see him and wanted to be prepared, but she imagined everyone was talking now.

As Michael pulled away from the curb, she found herself staring at his throat, and the bit of chest revealed by the missing tie.

"Does it bother you?" he asked after a few seconds of silence.

Oh, yes, it bothered her a whole lot, that triangle of skin.

"Everyone watching you being courted, I mean," he added.

"Am I being courted?"

"Two dates in two days is a good start."

When she didn't respond, Michael pulled over and parked. They were still on country roads with no other cars in sight. He reached for her hand and placed it at his throat, holding it there, wanting her touch as much as she seemed to want to touch him, then he leaned over and kissed her, a longer kiss than the night before, but still more tease than arousal—or satisfaction.

She tasted of chocolate and mint again, her signature scent, he decided. "I've been wanting to do that since I walked into your shop."

He got right back on the road again. She was quiet, too quiet. He'd obviously made a mistake ordering the limo. He'd thought she would be thrilled. Most women—

She wasn't "most women," obviously.

"Why do you drive to San Antonio for supplies instead of having them delivered?" he asked, uncomfortable with the silence. "Or ordering off the internet?"

"Um, fine chocolate needs temperature control, so shipping charges are high. And right now the weather's right, so I can bring it myself. Summer presents more problems. Plus, at the Sweets Market I can taste test new products. The owners are good about ordering samples." She turned toward him a little. "I haven't been completely satisfied with the white chocolate I've been using. It's good, but it's not great, so they ordered some samples for me. I'll taste a few brands today."

She closed her eyes. "I'm envisioning a white chocolate truffle with cinnamon in the ganache, then a cinnamon heart candy on top for Valentine's Day."

"I prefer dark chocolate over white," he said.

"Lots of people do. Some prefer the taste. For others

it's a caffeine issue. Sarah-Jane thinks white chocolate is a waste of calories."

"I have to agree. Seems like it's not even real chocolate."

"Officially, it isn't, because it doesn't contain chocolate liquor, but otherwise it's pretty much the same ingredients. Quality is the big variable. Good quality has cocoa butter. Poor varieties are made with vegetable fat."

"And you always use the best ingredients."

"Why use anything else? I want return business. Taste is important. And consistency. I know what I sell is a special treat for a lot of people. I like to picture the pleasure on their faces."

The Sweets Market was on the outskirts of San Antonio, so it wasn't long before they arrived. She'd called it a warehouse, so he'd envisioned a metal structure and high ceilings, but it was a converted office building made of brick. Inside, many of the walls had been taken down, replaced by shelving stocked with lots of equipment he couldn't identify.

The owner, Morgana Garcia, a tall, slender, maybe fortyish woman, accompanied them as they bypassed the stock of metal molds and assorted paraphernalia.

"You don't need any of these things?" he asked Felicity. "It seems to me that some of this might make your work easier."

"It could, but the results wouldn't be what I want. I hand form every piece of candy. If I used molds, they'd look uniform. That's not what makes me happy. I want every piece to look homemade because they are."

"Felicity is very particular," Morgana said as she opened a door. "She uses only organic products. She even makes her own powdered sugar."

Michael felt the cooler air at the doorway. Here was where the chocolate was kept. The boxes read like a travelogue—Belgium, France, Italy, Switzerland, several South American countries, but also American locales, New York, Chicago and San Francisco. The fragrance of chocolate hung in the air, making his mouth water.

"How do you choose?" he asked Felicity.

"By personal enjoyment and then by purpose, although sometimes I'm looking for something in particular, like for the Valentine truffle, which means purpose first, then what tastes best. Certain chocolates work well for one kind of candy but not another. I also have to appeal to a variety of tastes."

He was fascinated by her business persona. She was friendly with Morgana, but Felicity worked off her checklist, not allowing a lot of time for chitchat. He would've thought she'd be the kind to become friends with her suppliers. Instead she was just friendly.

"I set up a blind taste test as you requested," Morgana said. "I also got a few new darks this week and put out samples of those. I made up a ratings sheet for you. Take your time. I'll be back later. Oh, there's some bottled water in the cooler behind you."

"Thanks, Morgana." Felicity examined the table of products.

"White or dark first?" Michael asked.

"White. Want to be my assistant?"

"What does that involve?"

"Tasting." She grinned at him. "Honest opinions required."

"I wouldn't give you anything less than honesty," he said, making a different point. He cupped her arm. "I expect the same from you."

Her gaze never left his. After a few seconds, she sighed. "I hate shrimp."

The remark came from nowhere, so it took him a second to register it. "You do? But I ordered..."

"I know."

"And you ate..."

"I *know*."

"Don't do that again, Felicity. I appreciate that you were trying not to hurt my feelings, but I can handle honesty better than lies meant to soothe my ego." So, he'd started wrong on their first date by ordering ahead of time. He wouldn't do that anymore.

"Okay," she said, relief in her eyes.

Obviously, she was careful about not hurting anyone, an admirable trait, but not one he required.

"Now, what I need from you is just your reaction to taste, that's all. Which white chocolate do you like best?"

They went down the line, testing five different whites. "I like number two best, number four least."

"You have a good palate for this. Number four is a ringer."

"Vegetable fat?" he asked.

"Exactly. I liked number two best, too. That's what I'll order."

He rubbed his hands together. "Now the good stuff."

"This won't be as easy. There are different levels of cacao and sugar because of different purposes. You may not like something I buy because it won't be in its final form. Would you like me to taste first?" she asked. "Save you from eating the bitter stuff?"

"I want to experience it the same way you do."

She grinned. "Don't say I didn't warn you."

She picked up a small chunk, closed her eyes and sniffed it. If it'd been a glass of wine, she would've swirled it, he decided. Then she popped it in her mouth but didn't bite down.

Michael did the same. The fact her eyes were sparkling should've tipped him off, but he thought she was just smiling at him, happy to be together. As was he. But then it hit him, the bitterness in it, making his mouth unhappy. He looked for a place to spit it out.

Felicity passed him a paper towel. He couldn't get rid of the cacao fast enough.

"I don't like the flavor either, but it'll be perfect for a truffle I'll infuse with cabernet sauvignon. The chocolate has to be strong enough to match the depth of the wine."

They went down the line. Felicity gave him samples of only those she thought he would like. Next came the flavorings.

"Are you looking for something in particular?" he asked as she opened the first bottle, essence of orange, then held it up to him. "That's good."

"I'd like to make my own fruit purees, and maybe

someday I will, but for now I buy those ingredients. What do you think of this?"

He pulled his head back. "I don't like it."

"Women do. It's green tea. I pair it with Meyer lemon honey. I've recently developed a peanut butter and jelly, and not just for the kid client. Adults love the memories it invokes."

"I noticed that your candies have different tops. Some have an object, like a cocoa bean. Others have—I don't know what to call it. Swirls? Decorations, anyway."

"They're our clue about the content. The PB&J has a star drizzled out of chocolate as its identifier because when my sisters and I were kids and my mom packed our school lunches, she used to cut our PB&Js with a star cookie cutter. It's a wonderful memory for me. I do that for myself now. I'll eat the outside first, then the star part last. It just tastes better."

"I don't think I ever had a mom-made lunch. We always bought our lunches." Even so, his mother probably wouldn't have made PB&J. As children, they were exposed to exotic food from all over the world and were never allowed to be fussy about it. It wasn't until college that he'd discovered boxed mac and cheese, and ramen noodles.

Now *those* were great memories.

"My mother made the best lunches," Felicity said with longing in her eyes. "I never traded anything. She made her own trail mix. She even scored the skin of our oranges so they were easy to peel. To this day I cut mine like that. We all do, even my dad."

"My childhood is a blur," he said. "My father never

had time to vacation, so my mom would take us places, but with six kids, it wasn't easy for her. Mostly we visited relatives. I pretty much only saw my father on Sunday, when Mom put her foot down about not going to the office. He generally just worked at home."

She picked up another bottle but didn't open it. "Are you a workaholic?"

"Not like him. I get up at five, head to the condo's gym at five-fifteen, and am behind my desk at seven. I like to go in before anyone else—except Dad, of course. I can accomplish a lot more in that hour than the rest of the day. Otherwise, it's meetings or conference calls. Home by 7:00 p.m. I usually call in a dinner order timed to arrive when I do. I eat, pore over reports, watch some sports, then go to bed."

"Sounds like a workaholic to me."

"Well, I rarely work on Saturday."

She flashed him a grin, then held a bottle to his nose.

"Roses?" he guessed.

"Very good. My aunt's favorite rose vanilla." She'd reached the end of the line, everything tasted and recorded on her chart. "Do you clean your condo?" she asked.

He laughed at the out-of-the-blue question. "Of course I clean it."

"I mean you, yourself."

Ah. He saw what she was getting at. "No. I don't even buy my own groceries. I call in an order and it's delivered and put away for me by an employee in the building."

"You let someone else pick out your peaches? You

don't hold them in your hand and smell their wonderfulness?"

"I'm pretty much home for breakfast and that's all."

"I would get very tired of eating out all the time."

"The price I pay for doing a job I love. How about you? What do you like most about your job?"

She held her clipboard against her chest and smiled. "The wide-eyed kids. On my Saturday tasting days, I make cotton candy for the kids. You'd think they'd won the lottery. If you're here the Saturday before Valentine's Day, you can have some. I make it for all the children who come in that day."

He could see how important his response would be, but he wasn't going to lead her on. "I don't know how long I'll be here, Felicity."

"I'll make it worth your while," she said in a sweet, tempting voice.

"We'll see. What's the hardest part of your job?" he asked.

"It's more physically demanding than you might think. There are time constraints in candy making, so I often can't stop and give my body a rest as frequently as I should."

Morgana returned, and orders were put together. Boxes were stacked on a push cart and wheeled to where her preordered products awaited her. Michael drove the truck to the loading area and helped stow the boxes, as Felicity pored over the invoices, double checking, a frown of concentration on her face.

She was like a vacation, he decided. He forgot about work while he was with her, and she was both restful and exciting…and new. Fresh. Entirely different from any other woman he knew. Was it the small-town way of life or just her? Plus, her business acumen intrigued him. She was smart. Competent. He admired that.

She looked up and caught him watching her. Her smile came slow and brilliant. He felt like the only man in the world, and she the only woman.

He wondered then if long-distance relationships really could work.

Chapter Four

The scent of chocolate filled the truck as Felicity and Michael made the trip home from the Sweets Market, boxes filling the bed, a couple of special ones at Felicity's feet. Full from all the sampling, they decided to wait to eat the lunch from Estelle's.

Felicity leaned back, her hands on her stomach. "I am stuffed."

"Could it be because you ate about ten pounds of chocolate at the warehouse?"

"Possibly. And it wasn't ten pounds. Eight, tops."

He laughed. She loved the sound of his laugh. He'd been fun to shop with, had asked tons of questions and been a good sport about trying various samples, even those he couldn't imagine her using in a truffle, like jalapeño and black licorice. She hadn't bought those flavorings. Not because he didn't care for them, but because she couldn't afford to produce something that wouldn't sell.

"How long will those supplies last?" he asked.

"Beyond Valentine's Day, unless my predictions are off. People won't start placing advance orders for another week. At least, that's been the pattern. The day before is the worst. The day *of* is just mad selling."

She wanted to ask him to stay until then, so that they could have some real time together, not the snippets they would get. They needed time because Michael wasn't anything like Wyatt had depicted him. Nothing. He was attentive, generous and thoughtful. Where did that fit with "no soft core" and "hard-hearted corporate raider"?

She eyed him. "Why hasn't your cell phone rung this whole time?"

"I turned it off."

That gave her pause. Again, it didn't jibe with the all-about-business she'd been told he was. "You'll have a ton of messages, I imagine."

He shrugged. "One of the perks of being the COO is that people wait for me rather than vice versa."

Felicity just stared at him. She'd rarely had a date that was more than pizza and a movie. Michael had changed that last night, given her a memory. And today was more like a date than business. Plus he'd put his business on hold for her.

They were coming into Red Rock, back to reality. Even though she'd been working, it had been fun, too, nothing like her everyday tasks. Having a partner did make things better—

"I want to see you tonight," he said, giving her a quick glance.

"It'll have to be late. I have so much that still needs to be done."

"I'll bring dinner to your shop after closing. You have to eat sometime."

"Something light, please, like a salad. We still have your lunch to eat."

Michael pulled the truck around back so that they could unload directly into the kitchen.

"Did you wipe out their inventory?" Liz asked as they carried boxes inside.

"Just about. They had that rose-flavored vanilla you love so much," Felicity said. "Milk chocolate? A dozen?"

"You know me well." She patted her hips. "It'll be worth the calories."

Liz left to help a customer. Michael opened the cooler and divided the lunch, leaving her share on the counter, then he moved Felicity out of viewing range from the front window. "When I got back to my hotel last night one of your chocolate-covered mint patties was on my pillow. I would've known it was yours even without the True Confections wrapper." He nuzzled her neck. "It's how you always smell."

She smiled at that. It meant that tonight he would remember her, too, right as he went to bed.

He tugged her close, slipping way out of the businessman mode, holding on as if for dear life. He was obviously a man of deep emotion. He was so different from—

He backed away. "I'll see you later," he said, then he quickly left, not kissing her, and yet she had the sensation of being thoroughly kissed. How did he manage that?

Liz slipped in as Felicity stared at the back door, wondering what had just happened.

He'd been interesting to her before, but now he'd become fascinating. There were so many layers to him—the cool executive, the attentive date, the man who probably rarely heard the word *no*. And the lover. Oh, yes, the lover. A man so practiced and skilled she'd felt kissed when she hadn't been.

"I've never seen that look on your face before," Liz said.

"I've never felt like this before. Um." She tried to organize her thoughts. "Would you mind staying a few more minutes? I need to talk to Sarah-Jane."

"Go right ahead. I'll start putting away the supplies."

Felicity hugged her aunt, hard, then took herself to The Stocking Stitch, where Sarah-Jane worked as assistant manager, a title which hardly described what she did. She'd taken her MBA, combined it with a passion for knitting, then turned Maria Mendoza's little shop into a booming yarn business, both in the store itself and on the web.

Even when The Stocking Stitch didn't have customers, Sarah-Jane was busy, but because Felicity wouldn't be home tonight until late, she had to talk to her friend now.

"I'll see you at Tuesday night's class, Glenda," Sarah-

Jane said to a departing customer. "I promise you're going to love it."

"Hello, Felicity," Glenda said. "I was just fixin' to head to your shop. Will you be back soon?"

"Yes, but Liz is there, Glenda."

"Have you got any turtles? They're Tommy's favorite."

"Last I looked, I had a couple dozen."

"'Kay. Bye." The overhead bell chimed as the door shut.

"Your eyes look funny," Sarah-Jane said, rounding the counter. "What happened? I heard he brought a limo for you and you rejected it. Good for you!" She didn't slow down. "Did he lay hands on you? Did he—"

"He was an absolute gentleman." She gave Sarah-Jane an abridged version of the day, hitting the highlights, but not relating how he'd hugged her so hard in the kitchen a few minutes ago. Sarah-Jane would've thought Felicity was hooked too deep, too fast.

Uncharacteristically quiet, Sarah-Jane waited for Felicity to stop talking, then she said, "Sweetie, don't get ahead of yourself, okay? The way you've described Michael isn't anything like Wyatt said, and Wyatt's known him all his life."

Felicity was tired of having her judgment called into question. "You're not the one who's been spending time with him. I don't get it. Don't you want me to have the same happiness that you have with Wyatt?"

"Of course I do! I'm just concerned, and I don't want you to rush into anything you're not ready for. If Michael starts pressuring you for more than you want to give, can you resist?"

No, because I don't want to resist. There. She'd admitted it, at least to herself. For the first time, she didn't want to resist. "As I said, he's been a gentleman. He'll probably be leaving soon anyway. Maybe tomorrow. Who knows?" The thought cut into her, piercing and painful. Sarah-Jane was right to worry a little, Felicity thought. It had happened with lightning speed.

Sarah-Jane put an arm around her. "I know you've got it bad, and I know how that feels. If he invites you to his hotel tonight, don't go. Make sure it's right, not just physically but emotionally."

"I know." Felicity sighed. "I know you're right." She smiled weakly. "Time to get back to work. What are you and Wyatt doing on this fine Saturday night?"

"He's surprising me. I'm supposed to wear jeans, though, so it can't be anything fancy."

Felicity floated on air the rest of the day. Liz stayed on. Between them they got the stock organized and made a big batch of white and dark chocolate-covered pretzels.

She'd looked at the clock every few minutes, waiting for closing, waiting for when she would see Michael again.

And when she opened the back door to his knock, she went right into his arms, as if she'd done so forever.

Michael gave Felicity a one-arm hug while holding their bagged dinner with the other hand. He'd been working most of the afternoon, but she was never far from his thoughts. The feel of her now almost destroyed his control as she leaned back, waiting for a kiss, her eyes the brightest blue he'd ever seen, and filled with anticipation. He didn't kiss her even though he wanted to—desperately. He was trying to keep things slow and uncomplicated. He could see the potential to hurt her.

Even though he didn't just want but craved her.

A pleasant distraction. That's what he'd called her. He'd been so cocky about that with Wyatt. Now that he'd gotten to know her better, he knew that even if she begged, he wouldn't give in. She wasn't a one-night—or ten-night—stand. She was someone's lifetime. He'd been told that, but now he could see it for himself.

"How was your afternoon?" he asked, sliding out of reach and carrying the food to the counter, not wanting to see her expression if she was disappointed.

"Busy." She came up beside him but didn't touch. "Liz and I dipped enough pretzels to last through Valentine's. It's one of our biggest sellers."

"What are you making tonight?"

"Turtles. I sold out this afternoon."

He pulled containers out of a bag with the restaurant Red's logo. "Chicken tacos and chile relleno," he said, the fragrance of the food making his mouth water.

"That's what you call light?"

"You worked hard all day. I don't eat only salad for dinner." He saw her jaw clench. "What?"

"You really do whatever you want, don't you?"

She was so independent. He respected that—to a point. "I did bring you a salad. You just have choices."

"Oh." She looked sheepish. "I'll get plates."

He'd figured out a way to stay in town awhile, but it meant her involvement and agreement, and he knew it would be pushing her personal boundaries.

"Were you serious when you said you wanted to grow your business?" he asked as she set paper plates and plastic silverware on the counter.

"It's a decision that's hanging over me, yes. Do I pass up the opportunities that have been coming my way or do I stay with the status quo?"

"You're good at your work, Felicity. You know how to run your business."

She smiled and shrugged. "Failure isn't an option, as they say."

He'd heard those words so many times from his father that they were emblazoned in his mind, too. Consequently, Michael hadn't failed, not at anything that mattered.

"Why?" she asked. "Do you have ideas for me?"

"If you'd like to brainstorm about the possibilities, I could help. If you'd like me to take a close look at your business and give you my opinion, I could do that. It would mean letting me in on all the financial details of your shop." _It would mean I would have a reason to stay._

"My life is an open book," she said, her back to him.

He wondered how many people could say that and truly mean it.

She turned around. "But if I decide to expand, I'll do it myself. I made a business plan when I bought this business. I know how."

"I wasn't implying otherwise, Felicity. I happen to be good at that sort of thing."

"I imagine you are."

Her tone indicated the discussion was over. He knew he'd been pushing it, considering they barely knew each other. He'd only been trying to find reasons to stay on—or come back anyway. But maybe he should get as far away from her as possible—for *her* sake, he told himself.

And maybe for his own. She'd roped him in with her innocence and joy for life.

Michael couldn't remember a more pleasurable—or less stressful—evening, except for the previous night perhaps. Felicity moved around the kitchen, making turtles, answering his questions about the process but also enlisting him to help press pecans into the caramel.

"Finally," Felicity said with a sigh of relief. "I'm done. No more."

The building was quiet, the coffee shop having closed an hour earlier. She looked tired, yet she still smiled.

"C'mere," he said, pulling up a chair next to his, indicating she should sit. Then he took one of her hands and began massaging it. He'd seen her stop several times to stretch her hands. Her sighing groans told him he'd done the right thing. That and her closed eyes, and the way she sank into the chair.

He worked one hand for a long time, then the other, finding pleasure in giving her relief. He thought about the number of times a woman had given him a massage, and he hadn't returned the favor.

Frankly, he wondered why any woman had gone out with him twice, he paid them so little attention. A few women had even said, "It's all about you, isn't it, Michael?"

He wanted to give more than he took this time.

"Are you keeping to your schedule?" he asked.

She didn't open her eyes. "Check."

"What's on tap for tomorrow? You're not open on Sunday you said. Or Monday."

"I'm going to make you dinner." She finally opened her eyes. "Is there anything you don't like?"

"I can't think of anything." He'd stopped massaging her hands but was holding them. "What's your specialty?"

"Fried chicken."

His mouth watered. "With mashed potatoes?"

"And gravy." Felicity smiled with satisfaction, knowing she'd hooked him. The way to a man's heart…

"Then that's what I'd like," he said. "You won't be working otherwise?"

"Not on Sunday, ever. I'll work Monday, though, because of the holiday." She stood when he did.

"I'll plan something for tomorrow. We'll be back in time for dinner."

Not a question, but a declaration. "Is that an invitation?"

He smiled slightly. "Would you like to spend tomorrow with me?" he asked but didn't wait for an answer. Instead he moved closer, cupped her face and kissed her, a long, deep kiss that started slow and warm, then turned intense and hot.

"You always taste like dessert," he said, brushing his lips against hers.

"Without the calories." She enjoyed the feel of him against her body, against her lips. His hands were busy, too, pulling out the band holding her hair back in a ponytail, threading it with his fingers.

"I'll be flying to Atlanta on Monday, Felicity."

Disappointment slammed into her, shattering all the pleasure he'd just stirred up. She couldn't find any words. Was he leading up to ask her to go to his hotel with him tonight? Or spend the day in bed with him tomorrow? *You have one chance, Felicity.* Is that what he meant?

Could she resist him? Should she? She didn't want to be another in a long line of conquests, but she wanted him to be the one. Her first. She knew that down to her core.

Now he was leaving, and she was struggling with what to do about her attraction, and her personal convictions. She'd always felt that waiting for marriage to have sex for the first time was the right thing to do, a gift she would give only to her husband. But Michael brought out urges in her, strong urges. And she wasn't sure she could resist.

She took a few steps back, turning her back on him, heading to the cabinet where she kept her purse, giving herself thinking time and space. "I thought you still needed to talk to your cousin Sawyer before you could leave." Or had he already but hadn't told her?

"I've been putting it off."

"Why?"

"Because I didn't want to go home." He'd come up behind her, curved his hands over her shoulders. "I'm coming back," he said, his breath warm against her hair. "I just need to take care of a few things I can't manage from here."

"Of course." She pulled her keys from her pocket. "Ready?"

They walked to her condo hand in hand. The scent of impending rain hung in the air. She wondered if it would interfere with whatever he planned for them Sunday, make them stay home and inside.

"Thank you for walking with me," she said when they reached her front door. "I enjoyed the company while I worked, too."

"I don't know how often I should do that with your giving me samples to taste. And if I don't stop snitching extras."

"Did you? I didn't notice."

"Hence, the word *snitching*."

She was so tense she couldn't muster a smile. "What time should I be ready tomorrow?" she asked, staring at his chest. She heard a matching tension in his voice. She didn't want to see it, too.

"How about nine? I'll take you to breakfast at Estelle's first."

"It's a date. Or—" She stopped, hesitated. Would he return to Red Rock after tomorrow, truly? Or was he just saying that as a way of letting her down easy? Or maybe getting her into bed?

She made her decision—or rather, the decision seemed to make itself. "I could stay with you tonight."

Silence crackled in the air. She barely breathed. His

reaction came slowly, too, his hands tightening on her shoulders before turning her to face him.

"We met yesterday," he said, his eyes searching hers.

"You've never slept with a woman you just met?"

"You're different."

Was he turning her down? Rejecting her never-before-given offer? Of course, he didn't know that—

"You're different in a good way," he added. "We'll stay in touch."

Okay, Felicity, stop being such a baby, she told herself. He was right. They'd met yesterday, for heaven's sake.

She put on a smile. "Of course you're right. It's very sensible not to rush."

"It's not because I don't want to."

"You're absolutely right. I don't know what I was thinking. Well, good night, then."

That had been the most awkward conversation she'd ever had, she decided as she closed the door behind her. She covered her face with her hands, embarrassment filling her from head to toe. She couldn't have been more obvious. She hadn't quite begged him, but he must have known how much she wanted to sleep with him.

And he'd turned her down.

So much for the hard and cold Michael Fortune, whose heart had never been unlocked.

Just like yours. No one had unlocked hers, either, and she'd never been accused of being hard-hearted. It was just a matter of finding the right person.

Felicity went into the kitchen for a glass of water. What a difference a night could make. Last night she'd rushed upstairs and awakened Sarah-Jane to tell her she'd met the man she would marry. Tonight Felicity didn't want to see her, didn't want to share her embarrassment at offering herself—and being turned down.

A text notification chimed on her phone. Staying with Wyatt tonight. SJ

Felicity sighed. What a waste of an empty house.

Chapter Five

"Well, lookee here. The Suit's come back." Estelle plunked her fists on her hips and grinned when Michael and Felicity came into the diner, both a little damp from a light rain. "And he's brought Miss Felicity."

"Good morning, Estelle," Felicity said pertly.

"Mornin', honey." She aimed her gaze at Michael. "Still haven't invested in any Wranglers. You must be leaving town."

"Nothing gets by you, I see," Michael said.

"Your cousins are here. Wanna join 'em? They haven't got their food yet. We can switch their table."

Asher and his son, Jace, were seated with Sawyer toward the back of the room. Michael hesitated. He wanted an excuse to come back to Red Rock. If he spoke to Sawyer today, he wouldn't have a reason—

But they waved him over, and there was no way he

could say no. Tables were exchanged with a minimum of fuss. Felicity had met Asher and Jace but not Sawyer.

"Jace is a cotton candy fan," Felicity said of the four-year-old. "He likes the blue raspberry."

"Can we go to the candy store today, Daddy?"

"I believe it's closed." Asher looked to Felicity for confirmation.

"You come in next Saturday, and I'll make sure to have cotton candy for you," she said.

Michael watched and listened, not contributing to the conversation that ensued, trying to decide his next move. Sawyer hadn't cut ties to his father's company completely. Officially he still held the title of director of publicity and marketing. Michael wondered how long that would last—and how long Uncle James would tolerate Sawyer working from Texas. At some point, things were bound to come to a head.

Of course, the situation might be easier to figure out if James would just say why he'd given away so many company shares to a woman unknown to the rest of the family. A mistress? Former mistress? Polygamist wife? Blackmailer? Who was she? And what did Aunt Clara, his wife, think about it all?

"I've been waiting to hear from you, Michael," Sawyer said above the din of the Sunday morning breakfast crowd. "Figured I was next on your list."

"Let's not talk business. I'm enjoying my pancakes."

"Nothing much to talk about. I bought a ranch with my brothers. I'm not going back to Atlanta. That's it."

"You're still working for the company."

"For now. I don't know for how long."

Michael wanted the conversation over—and a reason to come back. "I'm going home tomorrow morning. I'll try to get more information for you. When I return, let's get together, you, Ash, Wyatt and me."

"You won't change our minds," Asher said.

"Maybe."

Asher shook his head but smiled. Felicity had taken Jace to the jukebox to pick out a couple of songs. The ease with which she interacted with the boy was enviable. Michael had no rapport with kids. None. His sister Wendy's baby was cute—from a distance—especially now that she was almost one and didn't need to be held all the time. His sister Jordana's baby was only a few months old. He'd avoided holding that one, too. Felicity made it seem easy.

She made everything seem easy, in fact. Here she was, holding Jace's hands and dancing to the cowboy music, her skirt swaying around her shapely legs, not caring if anyone watched. Creating a memory with the boy, Michael imagined. "I danced with the pretty lady from the candy store," he might say later.

Memories. Felicity seemed full of them, golden memories of her childhood. Michael had few. He'd suppressed his anger at his parents, his father mostly, for spending so little time with them, for not doing the same kinds of things that his friends did with their families. If it weren't for his mother, he wouldn't have any memories at all of Christmas. Even birthdays were no big deal. A check was deposited in his bank account. Or a car given. Or a trip to Europe. Nothing truly personal or thought out.

He remembered vowing once as a teenager, when it hadn't even entered his mind that he wouldn't marry or have children, that when he was a father, he'd do things differently. That idea got lost somehow through the years.

"So," Sawyer said, drawing Michael's attention back. "The pretty confectioner Felicity. How's that working for you?"

"Fine."

Sawyer and Asher exchanged humorous looks.

"You watch her like a hawk," Asher said. "I've never seen you do that before."

"She's watchable." Finished with his meal, Michael set his knife and fork on his plate carefully, precisely, reining in his irritation with the direction of the conversation.

"He's got Red Rock fever," Asher said, elbowing his brother. "We've been here for a month and haven't been infected yet, but he got it on the first day."

"I don't need a lecture on what a good girl Felicity is," Michael said, "and how I'd better not break her heart."

"No podium here," Sawyer said. "Or soap box."

"I'm enjoying her company, that's all."

"If you say so."

Annoyed, Michael gestured to Estelle that he wanted the check. She came right over.

"You're leaving already?" She tore off the tab and handed it to him as Felicity and Jace returned.

"I've got a full day planned." He peeled off some bills and handed them to her. "Keep the change."

"Thanks. Where're you two headed?"

Michael finally understood why everyone knew everyone else's business. They flat-out asked. "San Antonio."

"Yeah? To do what?"

"I've never seen the Alamo, nor have I been to the River Walk. Rain's supposed to let up shortly."

After a minute Estelle leaned close but spoke loudly enough for everyone to hear. "My guess is Felicity's seen them both a dozen times."

Chided for his apparent lack of creativity with regard to their date, Michael just gave her the eye. After a few seconds, she chuckled and left, not the least bit intimidated.

Felicity piped up. "It'll be fun going with someone who's never been before."

A long moment of silence ensued, then Asher and Sawyer started laughing. "You're way too good for him," Sawyer said.

Which was the truest thing anyone could've said, Michael thought. She was pure at heart. What was she doing with a man who discarded women easily, even callously, who was willing to play hardball with vendors, and even worse with competitors? Felicity often gave her lovingly prepared candy away.

"Don't be mean to him," Felicity said to the cousins, her smile easy. "He has qualities you're not aware of. See ya, *boys*. So long, Jace."

Felicity turned Michael's mood around instantly once they were on the road to San Antonio, entertaining him with stories of her childhood. As the youngest sister of three, she was babied by everyone, which was why she'd loved her summers with her aunt, who gave her some freedom and expected independent thinking and behavior.

"I don't recall babying Wendy, who is the youngest," he said. "I'm thirteen years older, though, so I was gone to college about the time she started kindergarten. We didn't hang out a lot."

"Do you think birth order matters?"

He'd considered that before, questioned the value of the idea. "Yes, but also gender and how many other children there are. And parental expectation. Maybe that more than anything." It certainly had been true in his case.

He pulled into the entrance of one of the most beautiful hotels on the River Walk in San Antonio. Felicity sat up a little straighter and looked around.

"We have an appointment here," he said, coming to a stop by the valet's stand.

"I hope it doesn't involve food because I'm still full from French toast and bacon."

He leaned across the console and kissed her. "This day is all about you."

She looked at him with the same tenderness that Sarah-Jane had given Wyatt that first day. Fire flared in Michael's core, then spread. He enjoyed the warm feeling until the valet opened the passenger door with a hearty "Welcome!"

You have all day, Michael thought. *Just kick back and enjoy it.*

He had her wait a distance away while he checked

in with the concierge, then they took the elevator to the sixth floor. She was wide-eyed.

"You haven't asked any questions," he said as they walked down the hall.

"I love surprises!"

He hated them himself.

He opened a door and let her precede him into a tranquil room, the hotel's famed spa.

"You're scheduled for an hour-long massage, with additional time just for your hands." The delight on her face told him he'd made the right choice. He wondered if what he had planned after the massage would make her as happy.

"Aren't you joining me? A couples massage?" she asked, looking bewildered.

"Maybe if we were further along in our relationship…"

"But I understand we stay modestly covered the whole time."

"I think you'll relax better without me there."

She seemed disappointed. How could she be disappointed? She stared at his chest, something he was coming to see was a tactic she used when she didn't want to see his reaction to something she wanted to say.

"It would've been really memorable," she said, then she put her head back and made eye contact. "Thank you. This was very thoughtful of you. How will you spend your time?"

Trying to figure out where I made my mistake, and whether the second half of the date will leave you just as disappointed.

"I'll go for a walk."

She looked around. "So, you were just joking with your cousins when you said we were going to the Alamo and the River Walk for our date?"

"I didn't say that." He bent close, making her come even closer, not wanting to leave her with tension lingering between them. This was supposed to be a day of fun. "I said I'd never seen them."

She finally smiled. She kissed him goodbye, then off she went, looking over her shoulder at him and laughing like some kind of woodland sprite.

He carried that fanciful image with him until he saw her again.

"My bones have turned to rubber," Felicity said to Michael when she emerged from the quiet depths of the spa later. "You may have to carry me."

Before she knew it, she was scooped into his arms and carried out the door.

Felicity gave a little shout and grabbed him tightly. She'd never expected anything so spontaneous from him—or playful. He wouldn't set her down, either, not until they were inside the elevator. There he kissed her—or maybe she kissed him first.

"My hero," she whispered against his mouth. When they'd first pulled into the hotel parking area, she'd thought he'd changed his mind and was going to accept the offer she'd made last night. Not just accept it, but turn it into something even more wonderful, far from the curious eyes in Red Rock.

Not that she didn't enjoy the massage and the

thoughtfulness behind it. But from the moment they'd pulled into the hotel, she'd gotten her hopes up, and some of her fears, too. The letdown might have been worse except who could think about anything at all during a massage?

She'd also tried to analyze him the entire time she was on the table. When it came to dating, this is what he did. He had a lot of money and he was willing to spend it to make a woman happy. The problem was, it took little effort to do that. Make a call or two and something was arranged.

Not that she didn't appreciate what he'd done, because she had. And it seemed important to him that she acknowledge that.

"Feel my hands," she said as they waited for his car to be brought up. "They did a paraffin dip on them. I have no aches and silky soft skin. You are the best—" She stopped herself from saying *boyfriend*. "The very best."

"After I left you there at the spa, I wasn't sure I'd done the right thing."

"I feel really good. Thank you." Which was the truth, after all.

A few minutes later they were on the road.

"You don't want to know where we're going next?" he asked.

"You have good instincts. I can wait for the surprise." She angled toward him. "Do you usually go on dates?"

He frowned. "Yes."

"I mean like this one. Where you plan something.

Where you do dinner and a movie. Or do you go to events?"

"I never thought about it that way. Both, I guess."

"Do you always do the asking?"

"Not always."

"So the women you date are forward?" She wanted to know if this was his usual way of courting, or if he was doing anything different for her.

He eyed her. "You are definitely from Red Rock."

"Meaning what?"

"You ask lots of questions."

"How else do you get answers?"

"You intuit. You assume. You guess." A hint of sarcasm coated his words.

"And frequently be wrong."

"So you like being right, do you?" he asked.

"I wouldn't put it that way. I like being correct, but I don't need to be *right*. Does that make sense?"

"It makes way too much sense. We should all take a lesson from you." He eyed her briefly. "Do you consider yourself adventurous?"

"In what way? I think starting a business is adventurous, but maybe you're talking about zip-lining across a river filled with piranhas. I would say no to the latter, thank you. Why?"

He pointed ahead to a sign indicating they'd arrived at Stinson Airport. She tried to imagine what he'd planned. "I didn't pack a bag, Michael," she said, curious and hesitant at the same time. "I don't carry my passport with me."

"We're not leaving the country, and we'll be back

in time for that fried chicken dinner you promised me. Have you seen San Antonio from a helicopter?"

She shook her head. It was on her bucket list. Not to see San Antonio necessarily, but to ride in a helicopter. She was so excited she could hardly sit still. She was yards ahead of him after they parked, having flung herself from the car, almost running ahead to the building.

"It's not going anywhere without us," Michael called out. "We're the only passengers."

She spun around, feeling her skirt billowing around her legs and her hair whipping her face. "I will remember this day the rest of my life, Michael. Thank you so much."

He hooked an arm around her and together they rushed to the building. Soon they were buckled in and up in the air. They flew over the incredible Texas Hill Country, across terrain that was lush and dotted with lakes. They soared over hilltops, low enough to draw gasps from her. She was in awe. The tour ended with a lazy flight over the city of San Antonio itself, the pilot pointing out the sights as they cruised over the downtown.

It was the fastest hour of her life. The best hour of her life.

He was the perfect man.

Except…there was no such thing as perfect. So, what next? He was leaving in the morning. How could she discover his flaws if he left?

Felicity didn't let those concerns stop her from being on a high the entire trip back to Red Rock. She couldn't stop talking about the flight, about the beauty of the land as seen from above. She wanted to know where he'd traveled, what he'd seen, and was enthralled by his answers. He'd flown in helicopters before, had been dropped in remote places to ski and to fish. He'd been almost everywhere in Europe, could afford to go anywhere he wanted, but generally only took long weekends instead of accrued vacation.

As Michael pulled into her apartment building parking lot, he considered their conversation. The truth was, he hadn't met a woman he wanted to travel with, not for more than a weekend anyway. But seeing Felicity's wide-eyed wonder at the places he'd been to made him want to take her, to show her the world. Maybe he would see things differently, too, appreciate them more.

He planted himself at her kitchen counter and watched her make her special fried chicken. She moved easily, competently, and wore an apron imprinted with pink poodles. She'd set a beer in front of him without asking and just kept smiling and talking the whole time she cooked.

"Where are Sarah-Jane and Wyatt?" he asked, finally realizing they had the house to themselves.

"I asked them to stay away until at least nine."

He decided not to ask why. "What's it like having a roommate?"

"It's great mostly. We've shared this place for three years now, so we're settled into a routine. You've never had a roommate?"

"Only my freshman year at college. I couldn't wait for that year to end."

"It's going to be strange when Sarah-Jane gets married and moves out. I'll have to look for a new room-mate or a smaller place I can afford on my own." She drained a pot of boiled potatoes, then mashed them with butter and milk, the final prep for the meal.

Michael found paradise at the first hot, crunchy bite of chicken. She hadn't been exaggerating. It was special. He told her that so many times, she finally put her hand over his mouth.

"Just eat," she said, laughing. "I can see that you like it."

The entire day had been surreal, he decided after they'd cleaned up the kitchen. The hours had flown by. Suddenly it was nine o'clock.

"Would you like a tour of the rest of the place?" she asked, giving the sink one last wipe down.

"The rest being?"

"Upstairs. My room."

"I'll bet it's like walking into pink cotton candy."

"You won't know unless you see it."

He hesitated. So far, he'd been able to control his desires, but alone in her bedroom? With her so willing?

"We'll have chaperones any minute now," she said, her expression all-knowing. They were both struggling with the same issue. Maybe they should just give in to it, get it over with—

The front door opened. "Do we need to cover our eyes?" Sarah-Jane asked, sweeping into the room, Wyatt behind her.

A moment of awkward silence followed. Michael felt like a kid caught with his hand in a cookie jar knowing Wyatt didn't approve. He was always in control and never at a loss for words, usually the right words. But in this situation? He felt out of his element.

"I'm going to head back to my hotel. I have an early flight," he said to everyone in general, then to Felicity specifically, "I had a great day."

"Me, too. I'll see you out."

She slipped her hand in his and walked him to his car. "I'll call you," he said.

She nodded.

Because she looked sad and he didn't want to leave her like that, he leaned against the car, drew her into his arms and held her, just held her. After a minute, she nestled closer, relaxing against him.

"Are you falling asleep?" he asked, stroking her hair, rubbing it between his fingers.

"It would be an easy thing to do."

Too easy. He could almost feel her naked beside him, their legs entwined. He let his hands drift down her, slipped them under the sweater she'd thrown on and ran his palms up her sides to her breasts. She sucked in air but moved back enough to give him more freedom, but he barely touched her.

This is what would've happened in her bedroom, he thought. And more. He might have shoved her blouse up, unhooked her bra, put his mouth on her and enjoyed her. She moved her hips against him and moaned quietly. He ached for her. Denial wasn't familiar to him, especially denying himself.

A car came into the parking lot, its headlights sweeping past them, but making them starkly aware of being in public. He gave her one last kiss, then climbed in the car and left, aware of her watching him.

When he got to his hotel room and saw the True Confections mint on his pillow, he threw his keys onto the bed, then moved to stare out the window. He started pacing, paced some more, sank onto the bed, paced again, his mind whirling. He poured a shot of bourbon and downed it. Nothing helped settle his thoughts.

He laid his clothes out for the next morning, then packed his carry-on bag. An hour passed before he finally stripped down and climbed into bed, first setting the mint on the nightstand, where last night's mint still sat. He hadn't been able to eat it, wanted to keep the scent of it around him. He grabbed one of the candies, the mingled mint and chocolate reminding him of her, the way her hair smelled after she'd spent the day working.…

He felt something unfamiliar—a longing for her to share his room, his bed. His life.

He reached for his cell phone.

"Michael?" she said, not sounding like she'd been asleep, either.

He wanted to tell her he wanted her. He didn't want to control it anymore. Couldn't. Everyone said he needed to be careful not to break her heart, but what about his?

"Thank you again for dinner," he said instead as the silence grew tense.

A long pause ensued. "It was my pleasure. Was there something else?"

He picked up one of her wrapped mints and held

it under his nose. "I didn't remember if I'd said thank you."

"You did."

"Good. Sleep well," he said.

"You, too."

But he didn't. He tossed and turned and then got up before the wake-up call he'd scheduled. He had a long day ahead of him.

"I won't lose another child of mine to Texas. Enough already."

Michael stood in his father's office, having just returned from Red Rock. He'd thought gossip flew fast and furious in that small town, but it was just as prevalent here in Atlanta. "Who says I'm moving, Dad?"

"I've gotten reports that you're courting a young woman from there."

Michael had been told all his life he was like his father, not just in appearance but in personality and drive. They butted heads frequently about business, Michael being more progressive, knowing FortuneSouth Enterprises needed to keep up with the newest technology. His father was slower to accept that, citing costs and staffing. But Michael had never allowed his father to dictate his personal life.

"I don't think two dates constitutes a courtship." Even though he'd declared as much to Felicity.

"Who is she?"

"A woman named Felicity Thomas, a candy maker." Michael sat, rested an ankle over a knee and leaned back. "How did you hear about her?"

"I always know what my children are up to."

Michael bet it was his youngest sister, Wendy, who talked to their mother every day. He'd seen Wendy only once on the trip, and then for just a short visit, but she'd delighted in revealing her knowledge of him having taken Felicity to Vines and Roses for dinner.

"I'm not leaving Atlanta, Dad. I'm not leaving the company."

"I would've said your cousins were solid at JMF, and look at them now."

"Uncle James caused the rift. He could fix it if he wanted to."

"Since James and I don't communicate, I can't help there. I assume you are?"

"Helping? Yes, he asked me to, so I'm trying. I miss them, too, more than I expected I would. I plan to go back there in a couple of days to try again."

Michael watched his father consider and weigh his response. At sixty-three, John Michael Fortune was an imposing man, even when he wasn't in power mode, as he was now. He'd seen and conquered a lot on his way to building his empire—to the detriment of his relationships. His children weren't particularly close to him because he'd spent most of their childhoods working. Michael's mother had raised her children almost single-handedly, with little hired help, a choice she made. Michael respected his mother immensely, but he believed she'd gotten short shrift in her thirty-eight-year marriage. Not that his father was abusive; he just wasn't there. Now that she had grandchildren, she took frequent trips to Red Rock.

His father, however, remained as elusive as ever—except when it came to business, and as if proving his point, he said, "We've got that Trexler deal coming up, Michael."

"I'm on it. I've done the estimates, the P & Ls and the prospectus. When it's time, I'll negotiate."

"Your head needs to be in the game."

Impatient with the conversation, Michael fired back, "When have I ever disappointed you?"

John Michael closed his eyes a moment. "You haven't. I'm overreacting, I can see that. I'm afraid you'll do what your siblings and cousins have done, and it worries me. When I'm ready to turn over the reins, I want you to be the one to accept them."

"You know, in the end, this is your company. You built it, then grew it into what it is now." Michael was beginning to understand his cousins' move in particular. After so many years without being allowed to even have one rein, the desire to create something himself was starting to hold some appeal. Until his brothers' and cousins' career changes—and now knowing Felicity—he hadn't given it much thought. "There's satisfaction in that, Dad."

"And twenty-hour days, and forfeiting a family life, et cetera, et cetera."

"Choices. Do you regret any of it?" *Do you regret not spending time with us, taking vacations as a family, creating memories?*

"I don't believe in regrets."

Michael smiled, then stood. "Thanks. I needed to hear that."

His father had proved a point. Do what you need to do, as long as it doesn't lead to regrets.

When he got to his office, he ignored the list of messages his assistant had compiled. He didn't want to have any regrets where Felicity was concerned, so he picked up the phone instead and called a travel agent he often used, one who would know exactly how to accomplish what he wanted, a date Felicity would remember, no regrets allowed for either of them.

Satisfied, he switched into full work mode. He had some catching up and getting ahead to do.

Chapter Six

Felicity didn't understand how time could speed up and stand still at the same time, but it had. She was so busy prepping for the holiday that she barely had time for anything beyond the basics of work, food and sleep—and it was about to get worse. In that sense, the three days since Michael had left had been but a blip in her life.

On the other hand, it also meant it'd been three days since she'd seen him. Touched him. It was a good thing she'd been in the business long enough that she was on autopilot, as she was now, dipping peanut butter fillings in dark chocolate. Her list was necessary and comforting. Do this, check. Do that, check.

He called once a day, mid-evening, giving her the break she needed by that time of day. But the breathing room she'd had since he left had also given her thinking room. She'd taken a step back mentally, acknowledging that everything had happened too fast, too powerfully. It was good he'd left. She'd totally convinced herself of that. Well, almost totally.

After a long afternoon bent over a worktable, Felicity's body told her it was break-for-dinner time even without her looking at the clock. She needed to rest a bit if she was going to start on her specialty truffles tonight. Valentine's Day was a week away, and the shipping date a few days earlier than that. Time for the big, final push.

Liz came through the swinging door and held up something for Felicity to see.

"This person would like to talk to you."

It was the business card of Morris Sheffield, the morning host for a San Antonio television station. "Did he say what he wanted?"

"Only to see you."

Felicity didn't want to stop dipping the peanut butter chocolates, not with only six dozen to go. "Huh. Okay. Send him back, please."

She tried to conjure up a mental image of Morris Sheffield, but his wasn't the station she usually watched.

And the man who followed Liz through the door would've been memorable, Felicity thought. "Tall, dark and handsome" might be a cliché, but it described him. Early thirties and built like a swimmer—broad shoulders, narrow hips, lean torso.

Felicity held up her hands in apology for not shaking his. "What can I do for you, Mr. Sheffield?"

"Call me Morris, please. My station received a press

release about a truffle competition in Dallas that you won. I'd like to do a piece on you and your business." He gave her a charming smile. "You wouldn't happen to have one of those third-place award winners, the truffles with the cayenne in them, would you? That one really piqued my interest."

"I'm sorry, I don't. I'll be making them in two days. I do have some of the first-place winner, the salted darks." She angled her head toward the cooler. "Please help yourself. They're on the far right."

She continued to work as he found and unabashedly savored the truffle.

"You've done that a few times," he said, coming closer, watching her create the star flourish on top that would identify it as peanut butter.

She smiled. "I started training when I was fourteen, so, yes, a few times. Did you want to do the interview today?"

"I'm shooting for Monday afternoon, to air on Tuesday."

Although it would be a boost to her business, it would be too late to capitalize on this particular holiday—or it could lead to orders she couldn't possibly fill, because Valentine's Day would come two days after the interview aired. She could potentially lose future business because she couldn't follow through.

Deciding the benefits outweighed the disadvantages, she agreed to be interviewed. "I'm going to be swamped on Monday. I'm never open that day, and so it won't be business as usual," she said as she washed her hands. She picked up the tray of finished products to put in the cooler. "My nice, neat little shop will be a shipping post, with packing materials piled high."

"Even better. Good visuals there, filling boxes. If it would help, I could get your background material now. Probably save us time on Monday, too."

She couldn't see any reason not to accept, just a niggling little thought that it could backfire somehow. "The shop will close in a couple of minutes, and I always take a break then."

"How about dinner? You have to eat, right? We can grab a bite and talk. Two birds, one stone."

Oh, he was charming. And slickly attractive. Not ruggedly handsome like Michael, whose smiles were rare and wonderful. Morris was polished and perfect— for television anyway.

"Sure, that would be great," she said.

"I saw a place down the street. Red? Is that a good place to eat?"

A lot of people would see her there, including Michael's brother-in-law Marcos Mendoza, Wendy's husband, who managed the restaurant for his aunt and uncle, Maria and Jose Mendoza, the owners. Morris would probably be recognized, too, by those who watched his program. That should cause a little stir in town, at least until the news spot aired.

"I just need a couple minutes to freshen up," she said.

"Take your time. I'll wait out front."

Felicity pulled the band out of her ponytail and brushed her hair, then dabbed on a little lip gloss. She looked at herself in the mirror then, saw exhaustion in her eyes. One more week, then she could go back to her routine. She would have time to sleep and time for Michael. For now, she needed to be not just professional but engaging. She wanted Morris to find the right angle for his story, because reporters always came with an agenda. If she could somehow dictate that agenda to the message she wanted to get across, having dinner with him would be time well spent.

Ready to go, she took out her cell phone and turned it off. She would focus only on Morris and the story, her chance to shine, at least locally. A comfortable business growth could come from that. She didn't want to get too big, too fast.

Felicity gave Morris a quick rundown on the town, trying to make it sound fascinating and lively. She pointed out The Stocking Stitch and told him about Sarah-Jane and her MBA and how she'd taken a small, successful business and turned it into a thriving, nationally known endeavor, selling yarn and knitting programs she'd designed via the internet. Sarah-Jane had combined her education with her passion, and going to work every day was a joy for her.

"Just like you," he said.

She smiled. "Absolutely." She drew his attention to the hardware store, with its hand-painted sign in the window, "If you can't find it here, you probably don't need it." Estelle's was on Felicity's list of recommendations, too, as the woman waved and managed to look curious at the same time. Potential fallout there, Felicity decided, as Estelle speculated on who Felicity was walking with, maybe even knew who he was.

Red was the place to be seen in downtown Red Rock,

a converted hacienda with historical significance from the days of Santa Ana, known for its top-quality food and ambience. Felicity and Morris were seated at a table by the front window. The bar was busy, but the dinner crowd wouldn't start filling the place for a while yet, so it was quiet, with classical guitar music at just the right volume to allow for comfortable conversation.

Felicity found Morris Sheffield charming but also practiced and skilled at getting answers. Whenever she tried to divert the conversation away from herself, he brought it back almost instantly. By the time dessert arrived he probably knew more about her than Michael did.

"What made you decide to enter the competition?" he asked.

"Recognition, for one thing. But I suppose I also saw it as a form of validation. If I won, that is."

"And you did. First and third place." He waggled a finger at her. "Don't tell me you were lucky."

She smiled. "I make a good product, but luck always comes into play, don't you think? I was lucky that those particular judges were partial to the flavors I created. Neither of them were safe, especially the one with the cayenne."

They spent a pleasant hour together. He took lots of notes, offered advice on what to wear that would film well. They rose to leave.

Just then, she spotted Michael at the bar, a drink in his hand. He toasted her before taking a sip. She couldn't judge his expression from that distance, but her heart leaped in her chest.

She walked Morris outside, excused herself and went back into Red. Because she was tempted to run to him, she made herself slow down, not wanting to embarrass him with a public display of affection.

But her pulse pounded and she felt a smile as wide as Texas coming.

If only he didn't look so serious....

"This is a nice surprise," she said, hugging him, relaxing when he hugged her back. "I didn't expect you until at least tomorrow."

"Surprise being the key word," he said, holding her hand as she sat on the stool next to his. "I thought I'd be here in time to take you to dinner."

"If I'd known you were coming, I would've waited." She couldn't get a handle on his mood. Was he upset?

"You were with Morris Sheffield."

"You know him?"

"He and my brother Scott were fraternity brothers. How do you know him?"

"He's doing a story on me and my shop for Valentine's Day. He'll be back on Monday to film it. Why didn't you come up and say hello?"

Michael jiggled the ice in his glass, then sipped what was left. He'd been caught off guard, slammed with jealousy, when he'd spotted Felicity with Morris through the window. They'd been so wrapped up in each other that they hadn't even noticed him. Felicity had been laughing, her cheeks flushed a little.

"How did he choose you?" Michael asked, holding up his empty glass toward the bartender, indicating he wanted another. "I'm sorry. Do you want something, Felicity?"

"No, thank you." She folded her hands in her lap. The light had dimmed in her eyes.

He knew he was being an idiot. He couldn't seem to stop himself. He'd arrived at her store only to find her gone, the barista and customers at the coffee shop delighting in telling him she'd gone out with an attractive stranger, not naming him, although surely some of them knew.

"Morris told me his station got a press release from the competition I won last month," Felicity said.

"But why show up in person? Thanks," he muttered as the bartender put another bourbon on ice in front of him. "In my experience, a producer calls and sets those things up. They may even go out in person, but not the reporter, who usually wants to keep things fresh, which is harder to do if his questions have been asked and answered already."

She cocked her head. "Are you angry?"

Yes, he was. He believed she'd been duped or at least misled. The situation smelled of his father's kind of manipulation, although Michael couldn't figure out what John Michael's intent might be. "Forgive me, Felicity. No, I'm not angry with you."

Her smile was soft and sweet, just like he remembered.

"Would you like me to keep you company while you have dinner?" she asked.

"I can order something to go and take it back to the shop. I don't want to disrupt your schedule."

"I think you should eat here, take some time to relax. I know you've had a long week, too."

He was so accustomed to using time purposefully that he wasn't quite sure what to do about her offer. The luxury of just sitting, eating and talking was rare for him.

"Let's get a table," he said, nodding to Marcos.

He'd already noticed that she talked a lot and quickly when she was nervous or excited. He was flattered by it, knowing it. She was good at recalling stories of interesting or quirky things that happened during her day, and the retelling was usually funny. She exuded warmth, so people felt close to her and probably said things they normally wouldn't. Like the story she'd just told about the woman who wanted to do something special for her husband for their fiftieth wedding anniversary, so she asked Felicity if she would artfully put together a basket of goodies to take along on their celebration trip.

The woman had brought in a frilly negligee, a pair of men's silk pajama bottoms, a lamb's-wool puff and a mix CD. Felicity added a bottle of champagne, flutes and snack foods. But the kicker was that the woman wanted a chocolate-covered cherry and a little blue pill boxed together with a card that said "Let's relive that glorious night!"

The risqué addition made Michael smile, especially because Felicity's cheeks turned pink. She really was an innocent, he thought. He wondered if that meant—

No. She was twenty-four years old. She couldn't still be a virgin.

He discarded the thought, even as he also considered

a fifty-year marriage. He'd never even pictured being married for one year, except in an I-would-like-to-have-children kind of way. He had liked growing up in a big family—and maybe he wanted to prove he could be a better father than his own.

When they returned to the shop, Michael sat near where she was making her prize-winning dark chocolate salted truffles. He enjoyed watching her work, especially because he'd learned at the warehouse about the importance of quality ingredients and working in smaller batches. She had a little cooling time between some steps, giving them a break now and then to interact.

He waited for the right moment, then said, "There's something I want to discuss with you. I ran some numbers to see the best way you could grow your business. While I didn't have access to your books, I could estimate based on percentages rather than actual numbers." He opened his laptop. "Here's what I came up with."

"So, what you're saying," Felicity commented after he'd shown her the basics of his idea, "is that I'm better off with a web presence than I would be trying to franchise."

"For now. And provided you're willing to put in the work. Growing a business online takes time and money, too. It means getting your name in front of potential business, which means getting your product spotlighted in important ways."

"You mean, like Oprah used to do with her favorite things episodes?"

"Exactly. It's no small commitment. You can't really go in half-hearted, dip your toe into it and see how cold and deep it is. You would need to dive in. So the question is, do you want to stay as you are or go big? What's important to you?"

One batch was ready to be dusted in cocoa. Michael could almost see her wheels spinning in her head as she thought about his question.

"I wouldn't mind finding a larger, steady base, like more hotels and spas. Work I can count on, month to month. If I have standing orders, it's much easier to plan and then there's also little loss."

"But the guests at those venues who try your chocolates will want a way to order some."

"I can handle that. I'm a boutique business, a special-occasion business, except for here in town, where I try to please all ages and cater to all kinds of events. I don't want to be hiring and firing. I like my location because it's right in the heart of downtown and within a popular coffee shop with lots of foot traffic."

"Then that's what you should do."

"I'm sorry you went to all that trouble just to have me be happy with the status quo, but honestly, Michael, you should've talked to me about it. I could have told you without your spending so much time on it."

"I was curious myself." Had he made a mistake? Overstepped his bounds? She seemed to be pulling back, not overtly so, but in ways he noticed because he was looking so closely.

She let him try his hand at rolling some truffles. It took him a lot more time and didn't look as consistent as hers, but they tasted just as good.

"How long are you staying this time?" she asked as midnight approached and she was cleaning up.

"I'll go back Monday." Although he might wait until after her television interview was filmed. He had a few questions for Morris Sheffield.

Michael came up behind Felicity, then began to massage the tightness out of her shoulders. She went limp. "What time will you finish up on Valentine's Day?" he asked.

"There's always lots of last-minute shoppers, but I don't stay open beyond my usual five-thirty."

"Good. I'm taking you out. Dress up and bring your passport. You mentioned you have a passport."

"I've had it for two years, but I'm still waiting for my first stamp."

She turned around. He didn't back up but put his hands against the counter on either side of her, caging her. She felt a little hemmed in.

"Are you flying me to Paris?"

He smiled. "No."

"Rome?"

"Not there, either."

"Should I pack a bag?"

"We'll be spending the night, yes. Is that okay?" he asked, his dark eyes searching her face.

"I need to think about it."

He put a little space between them, watching her.

"That's not the kind of thing you should just assume I'll want to do, Michael. I need to be asked. Invited."

He didn't hesitate."Will you go away overnight with me?"

"Why?"

"Why?" he echoed.

He started to move away, but she stopped him, her hand on his chest. "We're attracted to each other. I'm not in your head, so I don't know how I'm different from any other woman, any other relationship. But in my head, I know how different you are, and I don't mean because you're a bazillionaire or something. It's because of how I feel when I'm with you. It's poles apart from any other relationship I've had."

She flattened both hands against his chest. "And that scares me."

"If you say yes, what happens is entirely up to you. I only want to create a memory for you."

"We don't have to fly somewhere to do that. I don't need fancy."

He framed her face with his hands. "Tell me what you do need."

"Right now? Just you."

His arms tightened around her. His mouth came down hard on hers, as if he'd been keeping everything in check, waiting for this moment. She squeezed him back, gave as much as she got, tipping her head back as he pressed his lips to her neck and nuzzled, making needful sounds. She felt her apron being undone and lifted away. Then his hands curved over her rear, pulling her closer to him, letting her feel his own need. He unbuttoned her blouse, his gaze never leaving hers, then his clever fingers popped open her bra, his hands replacing it, cupping and supporting, hefting their weight, teasing her nipples harder than she thought they could get, aching with the full pleasure of it.

And then he added his mouth, his warm, wet, wonderful lips and teeth and tongue. She clutched his rear, dug the heels of her hands into his rock-hard flesh and muscle, and then her fingertips, gripping him, going up on tiptoe to better align herself with him. She tugged at his shirt, trying to pull it free, needing to touch his skin.

He clutched her shoulders, moved her back. "Hold on. This is going too fast," he said, turning away.

Felicity got her clothing back together, all the while hiding her wonder and continued surprise. She had power, she thought, surprised. She liked the feel of it, at least when it came to him, not to rule him but because she felt more his equal. He was a man of the world, and she excited him. *She* did. Felicity Thomas of Red Rock, Texas, college dropout and owner of a mildly successful confectionery was being pursued by—and falling in love with—Michael Fortune of Atlanta, Georgia, Harvard MBA graduate and COO of FortuneSouth Enterprises.

"I'll take you home," he said.

She took his outstretched hand. "I'm glad you're here," she said.

"Will you still take Sunday off this close to the holiday?"

"I don't violate that personal rule."

"Would you like to do something or rest?"

"As long as I'm with you, I don't care."

"Maybe a combination of doing and resting," he said. "I'll figure out something."

She'd never dated a man who planned before, who made decisions, who went out of his way to create a memorable moment. Or was it more about control? He liked to be in charge, so maybe that's why he was good at planning, whether it was a takeover or a date.

In the past, she'd been asked what she'd like to do, forcing her to become creative, then they did it.

"Is Sarah-Jane home?" he asked as Felicity opened the front door.

"She must be. She's got a cold. She ordered Wyatt to stay away so that he wouldn't get it."

"Better double up on the hand washing. You don't want to get sick with Valentine's Day right around the corner."

"Yes, sir." She grinned at his nurturing concern.

"It wouldn't hurt to take precautions." He kissed her then, a slow, lingering, tender kiss that Felicity melted into. "Maybe you should stay at my hotel until she's well."

The temptation was huge, but she didn't want to sleep with him—even just *sleep* with him—yet. "I'll be fine."

"I meant I'd get you your own room."

"Thank you. I'm good."

"I'll see you tomorrow. I'm not sure when. I have a conference call early. It could lead to others."

"No problem. And I'll have an answer about Valentine's night for you tomorrow, too."

He kissed her briefly. "Practice saying this. 'Yes, Michael.'"

"Would you two lovebirds quit already?" Sarah-Jane called out. "I'm trying to sleep."

Felicity stepped inside. "Why are you on the couch?"

"I couldn't get comfortable in bed. Hello, Michael. Good night, Michael."

He waved, then disappeared into the night.

"That was very sweet of him to be worried about you catching my cold," Sarah-Jane said as Felicity turned on a lamp. Her roommate was wrapped up in a quilt and had three pillows stuffed behind her.

"Do you need anything, Sarah-Jane?"

"Thanks, but no."

Felicity started up the stairs.

"Are you in love with him?" Sarah-Jane asked.

"Yes."

"Does he feel the same?"

"I don't know." Felicity stopped climbing. "Did you know? Could you tell when Wyatt fell in love with you?"

"I wouldn't let myself believe it for a long time, but I knew, on some level, yes. Do you?"

"No. I know he likes me. He's attracted to me. It's too soon for love."

"Yet you admit to being in love with him."

"I'm not a man."

Sarah-Jane laughed. "Do you feel the same as you did before? You still think he's the man you'll marry?"

"I don't know." She still wanted to, but she was being realistic. They were opposites in so many ways, important ways.

Felicity went on up to bed. She stared at the ceiling. He'd come back early. He'd missed her, couldn't wait until the weekend to see her. He wanted to take her away for a night. He wanted to sleep with her, she had no doubt. She wanted the same. But if she did, what happened next?

Did she want the memory of knowing him intimately or the regret of not knowing?

After a few minutes she reached for her cell phone. "Did I wake you?" she asked when he answered.

"It wouldn't matter if you had."

She could hear the rustling of bed linens and pictured herself curled up beside him.

"What's up?" he asked. "Do you have an answer for me?"

"Yes."

"Yes, you have an answer?"

"The answer is yes. Yes, I'll go with you." Her stomach clenched. She should've been more relaxed after making the decision.

"Felicity."

He said her name, just her name, but the way he said it—grateful, pleased, relieved—brought her the peace she'd been looking for. He'd been on edge, too, waiting.

"Again I remind you," he added, "that if at any point you change your mind, you only have to say so."

"Thank you." Just the fact he'd offered her that out made her more confident in her decision. "I'll see you tomorrow. Good night, Michael."

"Sweet dreams."

Seven days and counting, she thought as she drifted to sleep. It was plenty of time for all sorts of things to happen, good or bad.

Chapter Seven

"I want to try," Michael said.

It was Saturday morning, a few minutes before the shop opened for business. He stood at the cotton candy machine that Felicity had wheeled into the public area, preparing to spin cotton candy for the Saturday give-away.

Her brows rose. "It takes some practice."

He'd always prided himself in his competency at whatever he did. He was a natural athlete and had always picked up skills easily, so his learning curve was usually short and simple. "So, I'll practice. Show me how it's done."

She picked up a paper cone, swirled it around the inner circle, capturing the fluffy blue stuff, then she was done.

"Looks easy enough," he said.

"Um. You need to roll up your sleeves and put on an apron. Even then you'll still probably have it sticking to you in places that will surprise you."

He looked her over. In a few days he would have her all to himself, away from Red Rock and business and friends. Just them. "You didn't get any on you."

"I've been doing this for a long time." Doubt settled in her eyes, but so did humor, as if knowing she'd just presented him with a challenge, and he didn't back away from challenges.

"Afraid I'll be better at it than you?"

Her brows rose impossibly higher. "Oh, you're on, sugar."

Sugar. She used the word in a challenging way, but it struck at his core. No one had ever called him any kind of endearment, even in jest, as she had. He'd never let anyone that close.

"I'll help you the first time," she said, snuggling up against him from behind, holding his wrist and telling him how to capture the sticky sugar on a cone. He was center stage, with all the coffee shop customers and staff watching.

"Does it bother you that everyone's staring?" she asked.

She was trying to mess with him, and he knew it. "They're wishing it could be them."

"Or they're grateful it's not."

He felt her laughter against his body.

"You're right," she said. "One or the other. Okay, the bowl is ready. Slow and steady now, just like I showed you." She moved his arm. The candy stuck to the cone, then to itself. "Good. Pull up and twirl."

The crowd applauded. Relieved he hadn't made a total fool of himself, he used the final product like a king with a scepter, making flourishes in the air, then finally bowing to the laughing crowd.

"On your own now," Felicity said, stepping away.

Without her guidance, he discovered it wasn't as easy. The action had to be quick and steady. He was hesitant, and it showed in the massive blue goo barely hanging from the paper cone he held up. She was having a great time at his expense, leaning a hip against a counter, her arms crossed, grinning. It made him more determined to get it right.

He did get better, but not before he was a sticky mess himself, not only his clothes, but even his hair. However, he did get the rhythm of it, and she gave him a kiss of congratulations.

He would remember it forever, not just making the cotton candy, but also her laughter and encouragement.

Just then, the shop door opened and in walked every one of his relatives now living in Red Rock.

"Look, Daddy, there's that man you know," Asher's son, Jace, said, running to the counter. "He's got cotton candy all over him!"

"That's my cousin, Jace, and yours, too."

Chaos ensued. People crowded around, especially the children, who reached for the candy, tugging it out of Felicity's hands, sometimes hitting the child next to them, getting the cotton candy in their hair and eyebrows. Michael continued at the machine until everyone

who wanted it had some. Felicity made small talk, over-
saw his work and hand sold candy. Behind the counter
were two college students who usually worked at the
coffee shop. They bagged and boxed candy, as they
would also do on Monday for the shipping orders.

"Go visit with your family," Felicity said after a
while, bumping her hip against his.

"Have you met everyone?"

"I have." Felicity picked up a damp rag and brushed
at the cotton candy remains clinging to him. He'd actually worn slacks and a blue dress shirt instead of white,
which was a good thing. He'd left the tie behind, too,
and a soft leather jacket hung on a hook in the kitchen.
It was progress for him, relaxing his strict standards.

Felicity watched him join his family. His sister
Wendy moseyed over with her adorable toddler, Mary-
Anne, on her hip. "Are you sure that's my brother?"
Wendy asked. "Today he seems nothing like our father. There was a time not that long ago I would've said
he'd become a newer version of Dad someday, but I've
changed my mind. Or you've changed him."

"He's been very good to me, Wendy."

"And you've been good for him."

Wendy seemed about to say something else, then
stopped. Felicity liked that Wendy wasn't going to gossip about him. One by one, the various relatives came
up to her to say hello, but they saved their teasing for
Michael, who got slapped on the back, laughed at and
generally tormented. His cousin Wyatt tried to imitate
Michael at the cotton candy machine, adding a kind of
ballerina dance into his actions until Michael gave him

what Felicity could only call The Look, one meant to stop someone in his tracks.

It worked.

Felicity wondered if Wyatt, if all of them, had been as serious as Michael before moving here and falling in love.

Every so often, Michael would look in her direction and smile at her in a way that made her seem like the only person in the room. Then after everyone left, he wandered over to the counter.

"Thank you," he said.

Simple words, simply said. "You're welcome."

"My cousins and I are going to Red for a little lunch and a meeting. I'll be back later. Can I bring something back for you?"

"I'll just grab a sandwich here, but thanks."

"All right." He started to walk away, but she said his name. After a few seconds he came back to her.

"This meeting with your cousins? After it's done, will all your business here be taken care of?"

"Everything except the business I have planned with you." He made monkey sounds and scratched his chest.

She laughed. She'd expected a serious answer, a clue to where they would go from here—or after Valentine's Day, anyway.

He left it like that, just grinned at her in a way he hadn't before, then jogged out to catch up with his cousins. He looked years younger, she realized. That was the result of happiness, of being with family, of letting go of personal restraints.

Monkey business, indeed. She laughed, then turned

to a customer, feeling lighter and younger herself, yet with more unanswered questions than she'd ever had.

Michael sent his cousins ahead, saying he had to make a phone call first. He waited until they were out of sight then called their father, his uncle James. Being around all of them today had settled things for Michael.

"Have you got good news for me, Michael?" James asked.

"I've spoken with each of your sons. They're not budging."

"I'm disappointed. You always were able to persuade them and your own brothers to do what you wanted."

"That was a long time ago. We were kids. They're adults now, independent and competent. They didn't appreciate my interference, and I could see there was no way I would change their minds. Rather than lose their friendship, I decided to let it go. Until you tell them why you're giving away so much of your company to someone they know nothing about, Uncle James, they won't be back. Frankly, even if you tell them, I wouldn't be surprised if they stay away. It may be too late already. Why *aren't* you telling them?"

"That's no one's business but my own." His voice was filled with anger, and maybe hurt. "It's my company. I built it. I can do what I want with it."

"Then you have to accept the consequences."

The phone call left a bad taste in Michael's mouth. Even though his father and Uncle James hadn't been close for years, Michael liked his uncle, who had always been good to Michael and his siblings, not holding his strained relationship with Michael's father against them.

But both men needed to realize their children were all grown up.

Michael made his way to Red, where his cousins were already seated and enjoying a beer.

"If you ever break down and buy some jeans, Mike, remember this. You don't iron them," Wyatt said as he dipped a tortilla chip into salsa. Asher and Sawyer agreed, at first looking serious, then cracking up themselves.

Michael leaned back in his chair and let them play at his expense, wanting them to get it out of their systems. An empty pitcher of beer was exchanged for a full one.

"Are you done skewering me?" he asked his cousins finally.

"No promises." Asher lifted his glass. "To John Michael Fortune, Jr., who finally took that stick out of his—"

"Expectations," Sawyer said, elbowing his brother and lifting his glass.

They all drank to that.

They looked like cowboys. Or ranchers. Whichever term applied to them at this point. No one could tell by looking at them that they were wealthy enough not to work again, yet they had the Fortune drive to accomplish, to succeed.

This time Michael didn't make the same mistake as he had with Wyatt his first day in town. This time they all just talked, reminiscing about the good old days and looking ahead to life in Red Rock. They plowed through a platter of enchiladas, mounds of rice and beans and a bottomless basket of chips. They were raucous without being obnoxious, and the patrons around them smiled when they all laughed, their camaraderie contagious.

But the business at hand hovered around them, a thick fog of anticipation. As their meal came to an end, Wyatt finally asked the lingering question.

"Were you able to find out anything about the mystery woman?"

Michael looked at each of them. "I talked to your father. I told him how you felt, and also that you weren't going to budge until he explained what happened and why he's given those shares to someone you don't know."

"And he said it was none of our business, right?" Asher said. "That it was his company, and he could do what he wanted."

"Basically, yes."

"Yet you've come here again to try to convince us to go back at Atlanta and the company," Wyatt said.

"I'm here to tell you the results of my phone conversation with him, nothing more. I'm not offering my opinion anymore. You'll decide for yourselves."

Asher elbowed Wyatt. "He's here to see Felicity. He couldn't care less about us. We're just an excuse."

"True," Michael said, going along with it, although he'd enjoyed his time with them and didn't want to lose contact, especially if he continued to return to Red Rock.

"What *are* your intentions there?" Wyatt asked.

"Sarah-Jane told me you're taking Felicity away for Valentine's Day."

All three men stared at Michael, waiting for his response. As the eldest, who'd established himself first, he'd always been the unofficial leader of the bunch. To have them grilling him didn't sit well.

"I've made plans for a night she'll remember." One he would remember, too. "She's been working long, hard hours and deserves a break."

Asher and Sawyer seemed to accept his answer, but Wyatt wouldn't leave it alone. "Sarah-Jane would have my hide for telling you this, but I'm going to anyway. That first night you took Felicity out to Vines and Roses? Well, when she got home she told Sarah-Jane that she'd met the man she was going to marry."

Michael was stunned into silence.

"So, factor that into your plans," Wyatt said, not unkindly. "And consider how many pieces a heart breaks into when it's shattered. Some of those pieces never do get put back together."

Michael nodded, glad Wyatt had told him, and sorry, too. He had to give the trip more thought, his reasons behind the trip.

Not even if she begs you, Wyatt had said.

She hadn't begged, but together they'd decided to take the next step. Except, marriage wasn't the step beyond that one, at least not for him. Not with her. It didn't make sense, personally or professionally....

Although he liked who he was around her.

Michael saw her through different eyes later when he returned to True Confections.

"Why the serious look?" she asked. "I thought we'd fixed that." She set her hands on his face and smiled before rising on tiptoe to kiss him.

How did someone decide they'd met the person they wanted to marry after only a few hours together? Was she that flighty? Was this something she'd done before? Felt before? She hadn't talked about past boyfriends, long-term or otherwise.

But she'd said she'd never been in love before. Still, falling that quickly seemed…unstable and overly emotional. Emotional displays made him back away from a woman faster than anything.

Marrying someone like Felicity would mean trying new things all the time, being spontaneous and getting caught off guard in public. Here in Red Rock it wasn't so bad. But in Atlanta? He could lose his reputation, be perceived differently in business dealings.

"What's wrong?" she asked. "Did something happen at lunch?"

He should do the right thing and back away now. But selfishly, he couldn't. "Nothing. We're all going to the driving range for a while."

"That's great. I'll see you later, then." She said it with a question in her eyes.

He took off without saying anything else. When he met the others at the range, he hit ball after ball with far more force than necessary. He wished Wyatt hadn't told him.

Wyatt wandered up then. "Pretty aggressive hits, cuz."

"Uh-huh."

"Something on your mind? Or your conscience maybe?"

Michael gave him the eye but said nothing. He didn't want Wyatt telling Sarah-Jane anything that might get related back to Felicity.

"You promised not even if she begged," Wyatt said, moving closer.

"My memory isn't faulty."

Michael continued to hit balls long after his cousins left. He was stalling. He didn't want to sit in the kitchen watching her all evening, knowing what he knew now.

But it was exactly what he did. Felicity and Liz were a well-oiled machine, turning out truffle after truffle. Feeling helpless, Michael volunteered to clean up after them, although it took some convincing before Felicity would let him. She kept insisting he was her guest. He finally just ignored her, filled the sink and started washing dishes, finding an odd kind of peace doing it, too, especially knowing he was easing some of her chores.

His body ached from the misuse on the driving range, and several times he'd almost just left and gone back to the hotel, then she would look at him and smile, that full-of-light, pure-down-to-her-soul smile that had enchanted him the first moment he'd seen her, and it settled him. They were adults. They'd made an adult decision. He'd told her she could change her mind at any time.

So be it.

Chapter Eight

On Monday afternoon, Michael leaned a shoulder against a wall of the coffee shop and observed the activity. Felicity had been so relaxed yesterday during their trip to Corpus Christi for the day. They'd walked on the beach, then sat for a long time, not talking, just taking it all in. She was calm and content.

It was a far cry from the barely contained stress he saw in her now as they awaited the news crew.

She looked beautiful, like Alice in Wonderland, with her bright blue eyes and a ribbon holding her blond hair away from her face. A crisp, clean apron covered the lacy blouse and loose skirt she wore in television-friendly sage green. She made a pretty confection, he thought, as he had before, although not one made of spun sugar. She was stronger than that.

But she was understandably nervous. He'd led so

many major meetings and spoken to the media so often that it was second nature to him. She preferred the microcosm of her little world, not fame or fortune. He smiled at that. Well, apparently, she did prefer a Fortune. Him.

He'd studied her the day before, looking for signs of her feelings. If she had seemed obsessed with him or dangerously dependent, he'd been prepared to return to Atlanta. Instead, he'd seen a happy, playful woman who focused her attention on him but didn't cling.

Or maybe he wanted to see it that way—

The coffee shop door opened and in came Morris Sheffield, along with a cameraman and a young woman Michael assumed was a producer.

Michael shoved away from the wall, the movement drawing Morris's attention. "As I live and breathe. Michael Fortune," he said, coming directly to him. "How're you doing?"

"Good. Great, in fact. I see you're on the career path you chose years ago."

"This is my third television station. Each one's been a better market. How's Scott?"

"My brother owns a horse-breeding ranch not far from here. You don't talk to him?"

"He's living in Texas? No, we haven't communicated in years. Got our ten-year college reunion coming up soon. I'd hoped to reconnect with the old fraternity brothers I've lost track of. What brings you here?"

"Family business."

"Can you stick around after the shoot? We could catch a drink, although I'd kind of set my sights on the candy maker and thought I might tempt her away from her shop for dinner."

"She's busy."

Morris nodded. "I figured this wouldn't be the right time. I know she's got a lot to do, but I could set up something for the weekend."

"Let me clarify. She's taken."

He frowned. "By you?"

"That's right."

His jaw went hard. "Well, they do say opposites attract."

"Clichés are born out of truths."

Michael couldn't decide whether Morris was jealous, angry or frustrated. "Well, she's a sweet young thing. Congratulations."

Was he trying to imply she was too young for Michael? Maybe she was. Twelve years was a big gap.

"Why are you here, Morris?" Michael asked as the man was about to move on.

His brows drew together. "I'm doing a story on your girlfriend."

Girlfriend. That was a title he hadn't used before. "How did it happen?"

"The usual way. Press release, do a little research, decide she'd make a good subject this time of year. What're you getting at?"

"My father had nothing to do with it?"

Maybe because Michael was looking for it, he saw a flicker of guilt in Morris's eyes, but he said, "I don't work for your father."

"Which isn't an answer. He does own a major telecommunications company, after all. He has contacts everywhere, but especially in Atlanta. I could see where an ambitious young journalist might want to find a home there."

Morris stayed silent.

"Just make sure she doesn't find out," Michael said, low and harsh. "She thinks her particular skills are what drew you here. Don't ever imply otherwise to her."

"Hi, Morris," Felicity said, walking toward them, preventing Morris from responding.

But Michael had his answer. His father was trying to interfere in his relationship with Felicity, no matter how many assurances he'd given the man that he wasn't leaving the company or the city.

"You look none the worse for wear," Morris said, taking the necessary steps to meet her.

"I have my schedule and great help. I understand you and Michael know each other."

"A small connection through his brother...."

They went into the prep room, out of hearing range, the cameraman following them. Around Michael, the coffee shop customers eyed him curiously, then looked at the closed kitchen door and back to him again. He hadn't hidden his anger well enough, he supposed. The warning he'd given Morris had been quiet but direct, his words not going beyond Morris, but his expression open to public viewing.

Michael pushed his hair back, then walked out and kept walking, deciding he needed to cool off. He wouldn't call his father now because he'd be back in the office tomorrow morning anyway.

Why had he interfered? Had he offered Morris an incentive to woo Felicity away from Michael?

After a few minutes he ended up at The Stocking Stitch. Unlike True Confections, it was open on Mondays. Sarah-Jane sat in front of a computer but no customers were in sight. He pushed open the door, feeling so far out of his element he stopped just inside, not wanting to go farther.

"Michael!" She jumped up, started around the counter. "Is something wrong? Felicity—"

"Is fine. She's having her interview. I figured it might make her more nervous for me to be there." He glanced around the store with its colorful displays of yarn, then was drawn to a photograph hanging on the wall, a superstar actress wearing a bikini. The photo was autographed to Sarah-Jane from her friend, Adriana St. Clair, with gratitude.

Sarah-Jane came up beside him. "I crocheted that for her movie, *Texas Made*. Custom fit."

"Most men would consider custom fitting a bikini on Adriana St. Clair the best job in the world."

"So I've heard. I've had a lot of requests for special orders since then, and while the money is good, I decided it wasn't something I wanted to do. Too much time away from home."

He shoved his hands in his pockets. "You and Felicity are both homebodies."

"Yes."

He knew she was waiting for him to come to the point. Why had he stopped in? She had to know he had a purpose, even though he hadn't realized it himself until he was inside the shop.

"I'll make things easier for you, Michael," she said, "because you're obviously struggling. Wyatt told me he told you about what Felicity said, about wanting to marry you."

"I wondered if he would."

"Uh-huh." She came closer, looked him in the eye. "I was thinking I should tell Felicity that you know. To even the playing field."

"But you didn't?"

"I haven't. Not yet."

"Why not?"

"Because I asked her the other night if she still felt the same and she said she didn't know."

Her words landed like a hard blow to his stomach. What had happened to change her mind? What had he done?

"I see that bothers you," she said, a kind of relieved satisfaction, although not triumph, in her voice and expression. She was looking out for her friend, that's all. Michael not only approved, he appreciated it.

"You're armed with information, and she isn't," Sarah-Jane went on to say. "Because Felicity has gotten to know you in a way I haven't, I have to trust that she's seen an admirable side to you. Therefore, I've chosen to believe you are an ethical man, one who does the right thing. I'm counting on that."

"I can't guarantee she won't get hurt." Nor that he wouldn't.

"We all get hurt at some time or other. As long as it's not intentional...."

She left him to fill in the blank.

"She's not like anyone I've ever met," he said.

"'Different' can be fun for the short term."

The shop bell rang, indicating someone's arrival.

"Saved by the bell," Sarah-Jane murmured.

Michael decided to head back to True Confections, figuring the interview would be done by now. The TV station van was still parked out front, the cameraman stowing his gear in the back.

"It'll air during the seven o'clock hour tomorrow morning," Morris was saying to Felicity when Michael went inside. "Let me know what you think. I'd especially like to know if your business increases as a result."

"I will. Thank you for making it painless for me."

"You're a natural." Morris glanced at Michael then as he came up and slipped an arm around Felicity's waist.

"Good to see you again, Mike. Please tell Scott I said hello."

"I will."

As soon as the door closed behind him, Felicity went limp. "I am so glad that's over."

"But it went okay?"

"It felt good actually." Her eyes sparkled. "He bit into one of the cayenne truffles and his eyes watered. He couldn't talk for a few seconds."

"Wimp."

She laughed. "I need to keep packing boxes. What are you going to do?"

"I've got a flight in a couple hours." He hoped to get home in time to have a conversation with his father.

"Oh, I hadn't realized you were leaving so soon." The disappointment in her eyes made him think about Sarah-Jane's words, how Felicity had changed her mind about him being the man she wanted to marry. Maybe she'd just been getting Sarah-Jane off her back about it. Maybe—

He stopped the thought. He shouldn't want her to feel that way, because marriage wouldn't happen.

"You're going to be busy morning to night," he said. "I figured I'd just be in the way."

She took his hand and walked him to the kitchen. She'd sent Liz and the helpers on their lunch break.

Felicity looped her arms around his neck. "So, I won't see you until Thursday? Valentine's Day?"

"That's the plan." He couldn't stay, even if she asked. He had work to do, plus he needed to confront his father. "May I ask a favor of you?"

"Sure."

"Would you pack a small box of assorted truffles for me to take to my mother?"

"I'd be glad to. Anything else?"

He slid his arms around her, bringing her closer. "On Thursday, would you wear the red dress you wore on our first date?"

She smiled slowly and nodded. "What else should I bring? What kind of weather should I expect?"

"It doesn't matter much because we'll only be there overnight. Any chance you could leave before your five-thirty closing?"

"Actually, I could. Liz could oversee the last-minute crush of sales, and I'll get help for her. The deliveries will all be made by noon, so that'll be done."

"Let's plan to leave here around one, then."

She kissed him as her answer. "I'm looking forward to it," she said, dropping onto her heels again.

"Not more than I am."

She packed a box for him, then he gave her one last kiss. "I'll call you later."

Chocolate and mint, he thought, pressing his lips together as he walked out, tasting her. He'd taken his pillow mints home with him, indulging in one per night, thinking of her as he ate it.

During the flight home to Atlanta he shifted mental gears, leaving thoughts of Felicity behind and focusing on his father. They'd gone toe-to-toe before many times, but not over his personal life.

"Is he in?" Michael asked his father's executive assistant when he reached the office. He didn't wait for an answer, figuring she would stop him if his father was busy or gone.

"The wandering son returns," his father said.

Michael kept walking until he reached the desk. He leaned on his fists, looming over his father. "Stay out of my personal life or I will quit."

"I don't know—"

"Cut the crap. You sent Morris Sheffield to try to derail my relationship with Felicity. He wasn't successful, by the way."

"I did no such thing."

I'm not wrong, Michael thought. Morris had guilt written all over his face. "I don't believe you."

"Oh, I sent Morris, all right. He always was easily manipulated. Got him an interview at CNN for his trouble. But I didn't send him to break up your relationship. I did it for her. To increase sales. To help her become successful."

Michael straightened. "What?"

His father shrugged. "I had to check out someone who had you so hot and bothered. Figured her little business could use a boost, and I had the means to arrange it."

"Why would you be interested in her success?" Or failure, he added to himself. That could be his plan, too. Overwhelm her with business she couldn't handle.

"Because she's important to you."

Michael still didn't buy it. There was more his father wasn't saying.

John Michael came around his desk. He put his hands on his son's shoulders. "Don't you think your happiness matters to me?"

"I do, but—" How could increasing Felicity's business result in more happiness for him? Michael thought. He needed to figure it out, try to think like his father.

"There's no but. You're my oldest son, my heir."

But how would increasing Felicity's business make a difference?

His father dropped his hands and returned to his desk. "Are you ready for the negotiations tomorrow?"

Shifting gears took a moment. "I am."

"I don't have to tell you how important it is that we succeed."

"I've got it, Dad. It's under control." Michael wondered briefly what it would be like not to be doubted. Not to have his abilities questioned. He'd successfully negotiated the buyouts of three companies. That should count for something.

He headed for the door, turning around when he reached it. "Are you planning on retiring, Dad?"

"I'm only sixty-three."

"I mean, ever." He had no hobbies, no desire to take long trips with his wife as far as Michael knew.

"I'll probably die at my desk, son. Are you worried about how long you'll have to wait to assume command?"

He wanted to be in charge, wanted to make decisions he hadn't been allowed to make on his own. Resentment over that had been brewing for a while, he realized. "Yes, I am worried about it. Wondering."

"You have a lot to learn yet."

Did he? Or did he just have a lot to learn about his father's way of doing business? "I'll see you later."

Michael didn't go to his office but to his parents' house to deliver the box of truffles.

Michael had always thought Virginia Fortune was elegance personified. Her once-blond hair was now a stunning silver. She was as soft-spoken as John Michael was blunt. She gave unconditional love and provided a safe haven to all her children.

"Well, hello, darling. What a wonderful surprise."

His mother hugged him. The scent of her perfume alone comforted him.

"I brought you a gift. Happy early Valentine's Day."

"Oh, my. Truffles. How lovely. Do you have a favorite?"

He pointed to the triple chocolate. "Although I like them all."

They moved to the sofa to sit. After she raved about the chocolate, she settled back and eyed him thoughtfully. "So what brings my eldest child here? What's troubling you?"

He didn't wonder how she knew that. She could read her children's faces.

"When you married Dad you'd just started a teaching career a thousand miles away. Was it hard for you to give that up? To leave your family?"

"Things were different then. We didn't have partnerships like so many couples have today. Men were heads of the families, and women went with them, wherever they went."

"You didn't answer the question, Mom."

She smiled. "Yes, it was hard to leave my family, but I hadn't been teaching long enough for it to be my career, so that wasn't really an issue. Why do you ask? Are you in love, Michael?"

"I've met someone I like a lot, but I can't see it becoming more. She has her own business that she loves. I couldn't ask her to give it up to move here. She would have to start over."

"And you wouldn't give up yours for her?"

He looked straight into his mother's eyes. "I don't

know. If I left it would be because I wanted to do something different, not because of her."

"I see." She put her hand in his. "Your father can be difficult. Challenging."

Understatements, both. "I guess I want to know if you have regrets."

"I have six beautiful children, and now I have grandchildren. I live in luxury, never having to worry about anything. How can I regret that?"

She hadn't answered his question, but maybe she couldn't. To admit to regrets would make them real, when keeping them tamped down kept them at bay. She did have regrets. He could see that.

"If you could go back and change anything, what would it be?" he asked her.

"Oh, I'd probably make him be home with all of us a little more."

"He was an absentee father, even though he lived here."

"You know, Michael, if someone is doing the best they can, we can't criticize them because they don't meet our expectations. He provided, and he loves you all."

But he didn't make memories, not like Felicity's parents made with her. The stories she told—

"I hope I get to meet this young woman who's got you reflecting on your life," his mother said. "Can you stay for dinner?"

He saw it then, her loneliness. She would never admit it, nor would she beg him to stay, even though she wanted him to accept her invitation.

"I'd love to have dinner with you."

She fixed him melt-in-your-mouth pork tenderloin, rice pilaf and asparagus. He couldn't help but be reminded of Felicity in the kitchen, her pleasure in making dinner for him, her ease, her happiness when he told her how good it was. His mother was the same, taking pride in her work as a homemaker.

Taking pride. That was the major common trait he and Felicity shared. They both took pride in their accomplishments. The biggest difference, perhaps, was that she'd created her own business, built it from a part-time specialty business of her aunt into a full-time, poised-to-go-big company.

Michael envied what Felicity had done, but could he do the same? Did he really want to or was it a passing whim?

He had a feeling he would have to make some big decisions soon.

Chapter Nine

On Tuesday morning, Felicity, Sarah-Jane and Liz propped themselves shoulder-to-shoulder on Felicity's prep table to watch the interview on her tiny television. Liz provided the breakfast, Sarah-Jane provided the commentary and Felicity provided the nervous energy. She was in the middle, hands clenched and legs bouncing enough that Liz and Sarah-Jane each put a hand on her back, hoping to calm her.

"It's going to be fine, sweetheart," Liz said.

"Or you're going to look like an idiot," Sarah-Jane put in. "Either way it'll be over."

Felicity laughed—a little. They'd already watched two short promos, during which Felicity groaned. "I look ridiculous. I never should've worn that hair ribbon. Why did you let me do that, Sarah-Jane?"

"Because you would've told me to mind my own business. You're the one with the fashion sense, not me."

"You look gorgeous," Liz said. "The camera loves you."

"I don't—"

"It's starting," Sarah-Jane said.

"Welcome to Red Rock, home of True Confections, a candy shop nestled inside Break Time, which is a local coffee house. Master confectioner Felicity Thomas recently won a statewide competition for two of her truffle creations." The camera panned the display case, then focused on Felicity standing behind it.

While Morris described some of the candy creations available for Valentine's Day, the shot moved into the kitchen, where Liz and two helpers were packing orders.

"My hair looks spectacular, doesn't it?" Liz said, fluffing her curls.

And almost as soon as it started, it seemed, Morris wrapped up the story, Felicity smiled, then sighed. She'd survived the interview, which was not just good but great, at least from a business sense. He'd done a fine job of showcasing her creations. Heck, she would've bought some herself!

"Better?" Liz asked.

"Yes. I think I could eat now, after all." She picked up her bagel with cream cheese and took a bite.

Her cell phone rang a few seconds later. "Good morning, Michael."

"Well, how do you feel?"

"Relieved and okay."

"I thought it was excellent."

"You saw it?"

"I can find anything on television anywhere. You didn't look nervous."

"I was more nervous watching it this morning than when I gave the interview."

"That's normal. Look, I'm sorry this is short, but I've got a big meeting in a few minutes."

"I remember. Good luck."

"Felicity?" His tone of voice changed, softened.

"Yes?"

"I can't wait for Thursday. Bye."

Sarah-Jane rolled her eyes, having been standing there, watching. "Ah, young love."

"Exactly what I say about you and Wyatt all the time. You're pretty disgusting, actually."

"On that happy note, I'm leaving. You're not the only one with Valentine orders to fill."

The shop phone rang. Felicity looked at Liz. "We're not open yet. Think I should answer it?"

"I have a feeling it's answer it now or return a call later."

The phone didn't stop ringing all day. And internet orders came in by the droves. She couldn't possibly meet the demand, unless she sent someone to the Sweets Market and hired a staff of three to help. She and Liz could make the candy while the others covered all the different bases.

She decided to go full steam ahead. Sarah-Jane got someone to cover The Stocking Stitch. There were parts of the truffle-making process she could do well enough.

By late afternoon Sarah-Jane pulled Felicity aside

and said, "Either you stop taking special orders or you die."

She *was* tired. They were all tired. "This is a one-time shot. If I don't fill the orders, I won't get another chance at it."

"Do you really want to be that big?"

Did she? She'd been struggling with that decision all along. "I don't know."

"It's something you need to plan for. You can't just dive into it like this. You'll burn yourself out."

"I can't even think, Sarah-Jane."

"Then let me help. Stop…taking…special…orders. If people want to come here and choose from what's left, fine. Just tell those who contact you from now on that you were overwhelmed with orders after the interview, then give them a discount code to apply to another purchase down the road."

Which is what they did. Even so, they were up all night. She hired someone to make deliveries in San Antonio and the surrounding communities the next day, then she and her crew started on the chocolate-dipped strawberries, the unavoidably last-minute item. By the time Valentine's Day arrived, she'd gotten about six hours' sleep over two days.

Then Michael arrived.

She was so tired she almost fell into his arms and sobbed.

Michael saw how fragile she looked. "Is everything under control here?" he asked Liz.

"As of a few minutes ago, yes. Relatively so, anyway, compared to the past two days."

"Can she leave?"

"I'm not done yet," Felicity said, straightening, lifting her chin.

"Yes, you are, sweetheart," Liz said, passing Felicity's purse to her. "Take her, Michael. Have fun."

Felicity eyed him, saw what he was wearing. "That's not my Michael. He's not wearing a suit. He's got on… khakis. And a sport shirt. I don't know this man." She grinned stupidly as he pulled her along.

My Michael. The words were music to his ears. "Have you packed?" he asked as he opened his car door for her.

"I haven't even been home for two days." She looked at him with glazed eyes. "I need a shower."

"All right." He silently cursed his father for putting her in this position. She had plenty of business without the extra resulting from the interview.

"The power of the media," she murmured, closing her eyes and resting her head.

"And being the new, hot item."

"Who would've thought? I expected an increase. I didn't expect what I got."

My father knew. Morris knew.

"I hope I'll be good company for you," she said, her voice drifting.

"You'll have time to sleep on the plane."

That roused her. "Plane?"

"I hired Tanner Redmond." He was a local charter pilot who'd married Michael's sister Jordana the year before. "He's flying us to the Cayman Islands."

Felicity's eyes opened. She sat up. "He is? We're going to the Caribbean?"

"Happy Valentine's Day." She liked adventure and memories? He would provide them for her.

She smiled giddily. He'd missed her. Even though he'd been consumed with the buyout, he'd missed her, had wished she was at his house at night to talk to, to let down. Instead he'd been keyed up, and still angry at his father for interfering in Felicity's life. He needed this night away, too. Maybe they could turn it into more than one....

At her apartment, Michael paced while she packed. "You don't need that much," he called up the staircase, wondering if she'd fallen asleep.

She came down dressed in a summer dress and sandals, suitcase in hand, a much larger one that he thought she needed, but that was a woman for you. At the bottom of the stairs, he reached for it but she didn't let go.

"You haven't kissed me hello," she said.

He slowed himself down, stopped being in such a hurry to get away. "How remiss of me."

"I thought so, too."

Even worn out, she sparkled, her eyes bright, her lips tempting. He moved in on her in such a way that she laughed. He acted as if he was going to devour her, then shifted gears and kissed her tenderly and fully so that when he lifted his head, her eyes were still closed, her mouth upturned in a smile. She sighed.

"Now *that* is a Happy Valentine's Day greeting," she said. "We can go."

He opened her front door. "There's more where that came from."

"I'm counting on it."

Michael's brother-in-law Tanner Redmond was the owner/operator of Redmond Flight School. His close-cropped hair was a carryover from his days in the air force. He'd made his own success since getting out, was a trusted charter pilot and instructor. Even if they hadn't been related, Michael would've hired him by reputation alone.

"How long is the flight?" Felicity asked Michael, as they buckled in.

"Not that long. We'll be there in plenty of time to enjoy dinner at sunset. Tanner's made up a couple of the seats as a bed for you."

Her brows went up. "There's a bed? Are we going to be a mile high?"

He gave her a steady look, hiding his sudden surge in anticipation. "We're not going to be anywhere if you don't get some sleep first."

"Spoilsport."

He traced a finger down her neck, then hooked the bodice of her sundress. "I'd be happy—more than happy—to accommodate any wishes you have. Just be sure, Felicity."

She sucked in a breath as he slipped a hand under her dress to cup her breast, her nipple grazing his fingertips, then pressing into his palm.

"We're all set up here" came Tanner's voice through the speakers. "Arc you ready?"

Michael pressed the intercom button overhead, staring at Felicity. "More than ready."

"Okay. I'll let you know when you can go to bed."

Michael shook his head at Felicity, who seemed ready to add her own double entendres.

The anticipation would build steadily now, he thought, satisfied. He liked anticipation almost as much as he liked a payoff.

He reached for her hand, then as the plane barreled down the short runway, she squeezed his hard.

"Don't like to fly?"

"I haven't taken that many flights and never one in a plane this small." She glanced around the interior, then back at him. "You look nice in your casual wear. Did you go shopping just for this trip?"

"As a matter of fact, I did."

"You seem more approachable. Or maybe that's because you don't look so stern right now."

"How can anyone be stern around you?" He brushed his fingers down her hair, tucking it behind her ear before he pressed his lips to the sensitive spot behind her lobe.

"Are you seducing me?" she asked, a little breathless.

"If you have to ask, it's not working."

It wasn't long before Tanner turned off the fasten-seat-belt sign. Michael got up immediately and moved Felicity to the made-up bed. He folded back the blanket and fluffed a pillow.

"What, no mint?" she asked.

"You should hit Tanner up for the business."

"I'll do that." She settled in. "Stay with me, please."

He didn't have to be asked twice. Two seats had been prepared, so there was room for both of them. He kicked off his shoes and stretched out beside her, on top of the blanket. She snuggled close, pressed her face against his shoulder, rested an arm across his chest. He entwined his fingers with hers.

"The faster you fall sleep, the sooner we get there," he said.

"You sound just like my father. Those family vacations were so much fun...." Her voice trailed off.

Fastest fall into sleep ever, he decided. The next thing he heard was Tanner announcing ten minutes until landing.

She opened her eyes, saw him and smiled. "Hi."

He brushed his fingers along her cheek. "Next stop, paradise."

They resettled in their upright seats and held hands while they landed, refreshed, rested and ready for whatever happened next.

Chapter Ten

"The suite has two bedrooms," Michael said from behind Felicity when they entered their spacious ground-floor hotel room in the luxurious resort on Seven Mile Beach. She could see a patio, where a table for two was set for dinner. Beyond that, just sand and sea.

"We have an hour and a half until they serve us." He walked past her with her suitcase, taking it to one bedroom and setting it inside the door. Then he came back for his and took it to the other bedroom.

The fact he continued to give her an out if she wanted it endeared him to her all the more.

"This is the most beautiful place I've ever been," she said, kicking off her sandals and heading outside. She moved past the table and onto the cool sand that engulfed her feet and squished between her toes. It was a short walk to the water from there, but she was drawn powerfully to it. She wished they were staying a week. Maybe they could. Maybe the night would lead to something they hadn't planned on.

She turned around, walking backward, making sure he was coming, too. He was right there, his shoes off, pant legs rolled up. He looked years younger and carefree. She held out her hand. He took it and they ran straight into the sea. She laughed at the feel of the water, not warm but not really cold, either. The waves were gentle.

"Did you pack a bathing suit?" he asked.

"Yes. Did you?"

"This answer may surprise you, but yes, I did."

"What are we waiting for?"

They hurried back to their rooms, changed and met on the patio. Everything about him appealed to her. His body was strong and sturdy and muscular, his chest dusted with dark hair that made a fascinating trail down his stomach to his abdomen, disappearing beneath his trunks. She didn't want to swim. She wanted to haul him to bed and kiss him senseless, then have her way with him.

"You're wearing a Sarah-Jane original," he said, openly admiring her hot-pink crocheted bikini.

Felicity had never thought she would wear the daring Christmas gift that barely covered her rear, that cupped and lifted her breasts, giving her cleavage she didn't realize she had until she put on the suit.

"Do you like it?" she asked coyly, turning around slowly, giving him a full view.

"You take my breath away."

"I'm in need of a little oxygen myself," she said, slipping her arms around him, coming body to body. She spread her hands on his chest and explored the tautness and textures, pressing her lips to his flesh, sweeping her tongue along his ribs. She felt him grow hard against her belly, heard him make sounds of need—or maybe pleasure, felt his fingers dig into her back, encouraging her to move lower until she swirled her tongue around his navel.

He gripped her shoulders and hauled her up, bringing his mouth down hard on hers, sliding his hands under her bikini bottom and grabbing her rear, squeezing, then smoothing over and over, lifting her to him—

A whistle pierced the air. Three teenage boys were skimboarding along the shore. Whether the whistle had been intended to let Felicity and Michael know they had an audience, or they were whistling at each other didn't matter. They pushed apart instantly, both breathing heavily.

"That was somewhat nice," she said after a minute, giving him a wink.

"Brat." He hooked his arm around her, and they walked to the shore, the boys having moved on.

They held hands and eased into the water, gentle waves lapping at their feet, their ankles. She'd only been swimming in the ocean once. She had a healthy fear and respect for its power. She looked back toward shore. Other than the boys earlier, there didn't seem to be anyone around. "Why are we relatively alone here?"

"I requested it."

"Do you always get what you ask for?"

He frowned. "I guess so. I'm not sure I ever gave it much thought. Most people don't ask for something they aren't pretty sure they'll get."

She thought that over for a few seconds. "I think people get turned down all the time. You're just charmed." And rich. Rich helped, she supposed. It wasn't the answer to everything in life, but for acquiring *things* it was.

"There's a difference, too, between getting what you ask for and getting what you want."

"That's a very good point, Mr. Fortune." A larger wave rolled in on them. She closed her eyes and jumped, never letting go of his hand.

They played awhile longer, having water fights, taking every opportunity to touch each other. *Fever pitch.* She finally understood the term.

They showered separately. She put on her red dress and went barefoot. She felt sexy and liberated, especially when she saw him standing on the patio, waiting for her. She loved him, was ready for him. For this intimacy.

A cart had been rolled in, with glasses and a pitcher of strawberry margaritas. He met her in the living room, taking her hand and kissing it, then tucking her arm under his, walking her to a cushioned love seat. He poured their drinks, then sat beside her.

The sun touched the water. In short order it sizzled below the horizon as they sipped their sweet concoctions.

"Another unforgettable moment," she said, and felt him kiss her head, his breath warm against her hair.

The food arrived. He hadn't ordered fancy, but a chicken fettuccini with asparagus, and a rustic pizza with rosemary, prosciutto and arugula drizzled with truffle oil. They shared everything, including a plate of tropical fruit for dessert, each piece perfect and sweet.

Then it was time.

Michael rolled the cart into the hall, put the do-not-disturb sign on the doorknob, anticipation having reached the point of no return. She could still say no and he would stop, but he didn't think she planned to say no. The memory of her in the bikini was all he could see. Did she have a similar image of him? Bathing suits left little to the imagination, especially when wet. Or a second skin, like hers was.

He found her standing in the open patio door, watching the sea. He came up behind her, wrapping his arms around her, resting his jaw along her hair.

"Would you like to take a walk?" he asked.

"No."

"Would you like to dance?"

It took her a little longer to answer. "No." She turned to face him. "I would like you to take me to your bed."

He scooped her into his arms. "See? You get what you ask for."

He'd already turned down his bedding, folding all of it to the bottom of the bed. He'd lowered the lights, but left some on, too, wanting to see her face as they made love, wanted her to see him. He wanted to stretch out beside her, to get his fill of her, to touch, to feel, to kiss. He wanted her hair to drift against his skin.

He wanted it all. Now.

Michael set her down next to the bed. She was shaking. Nerves or eagerness? He felt the same, although why he was nervous was beyond him. He cupped her face, kissed her with as much restraint as he could manage. *You're making a memory,* he reminded himself. *You only get one chance at a first time.*

He felt her arms come between them but only to unbutton his shirt.

"I feel like I've been waiting years for this, for you," she said, breathing hot air against the skin she revealed as she continued down his shirt. She shoved it off his shoulders, letting it drop, then her hands and mouth were everywhere. When she reached for the zipper of his pants, he unzipped her dress, encountering nothing under it, no bra, no panties, just smooth, silky skin and toned, perfectly curved flesh.

She shoved his pants down as her dress fell to the floor. "You are spectacular," she said, barely audible, as she wrapped her shaking hands around him.

"You stole my line." Her breasts were perfect, her nipples hard, inviting his mouth. He took her hands away from him, held them to her sides, needing more control. Then he had her on her back on the bed, was covering her with his own body. They stayed like that, not moving, just feeling. She had her eyes closed and sucked air through her teeth. Her body shook.

"Do I need protection?" he asked.

"I'm on the Pill."

Still, he didn't want to rush it. He moved onto his side so that he could touch her everywhere. He angled a leg between hers, nudging them open, giving him access.

He touched her, that's all, just barely touched her and she was arching high, pressing into his hand. He wanted to be inside her the first time, so before she peaked he moved above her, positioned himself. Her breath came out unsteady and shallow. Her eyes were open wide, watching him as he pressed forward, as ready as she.

Except…he found resistance. He knew she was ready, so he pressed some more, and found more resistance.

And then he knew. Was shocked—and yet not. "Are you a virgin?"

She nodded. "I want this. You. *Please*."

He couldn't take it all in, not positioned as he was. Not as ready as he was. He rolled to the side of the bed and sat up. "Why didn't you tell me?" he asked over his shoulder.

"Does it really make that much of a difference?"

"Of course it does, especially at our ages. There's a responsibility attached." An obligation, he thought. They weren't young and foolish. They were mature… and foolish. "This is not how your first time should be."

He reached for his phone and left the room in all his glorious nakedness.

Felicity watched him go without a word, shutting the bedroom door behind him. She pulled the sheet up, raised her knees and rested her forehead against them. She'd messed up. He was right—she should've told him, although she didn't think he should have stopped. Not at that point. It couldn't have been easy for him—

She covered her face with her hands as tears pressed at her eyes, burning with embarrassment. He must hate her. He was probably trying to get Tanner to fly them home right now.

She got out of bed, reached for her dress, wanting to leave his room and hide out in her own, but then the door opened and he strode in, looking like the executive he was, although a naked one. She wouldn't want to tangle with him in a boardroom, not with that expression on his face. But tangling under the sheets…

She held the dress against her body, swiped at her tears. She saw his gaze soften a little.

"You need to get dressed," he said. "We're getting married."

"What?" She backed up. "We are not."

"Correct me if I'm wrong, but I think you're a virgin because you made a conscious decision to wait for marriage. Right or wrong?"

"Right, but—"

"Then we're getting married." He opened his closet door.

She jerked on her dress while he had his back turned, then marched up to him. "You can't just tell me we're getting married and expect me to obey, Michael Fortune."

He aimed a steady, fierce look at her, one that said "Don't lie to me." "Why did you decide to sleep with me, Felicity?"

"Because you're the one," she fired back.

"What does that mean?"

"I never wanted anyone before you, not enough to actually do it. You think it was hard to stay a virgin all these years? It wasn't. But you're different."

"How? Tell me exactly how."

She lifted her chin. She wasn't going to be accused of lying to him or withholding information again. "Because I'm in love with you."

He turned his head away so fast, she didn't get to see his reaction. "Then it's settled. Go get ready."

"No."

"I don't want to fight, Felicity."

"I won't marry you until you answer a question for me. Why are *you* doing this? Why marry me?"

"Because I want to sleep with you."

She tried to see deeper. "But I'm willing to sleep with you without marriage."

"You would regret it."

She frowned. "That would be my problem, not yours."

"You don't get it." He cupped her shoulders. "I want you more than anyone ever. I've wanted you from the moment you walked into Estelle's."

All she could see were hurdles. Where would they live? Who would give up their career? Did he want children? She did. And did he really think they could sustain a marriage on lust alone?

He must love her and not be willing to admit it, even to himself. Surely Michael wouldn't ever do anything he didn't want to, didn't choose to do. And surely he knew a marriage couldn't be built on such a shaky foundation.

No matter what he said, she could walk away right now, she had no doubt of that. He wouldn't force her.

But you want to be his wife. The words whispering in her head made the decision for her. She would make it work. He loved her, she was sure of it. She just had to get him to admit it. She hadn't failed at anything important. This marriage would be no different.

And heaven help her, she wanted to be married to him, no matter what the circumstance.

"I'll get ready," she said, laying a hand along his face and giving him a tender kiss.

Because the red dress was the most formal garment she'd brought, and because he liked it so much, she decided to wear it. If she felt twinges about going through with the ceremony without her family and friends there to wish her well, she would just have to ignore them. And she'd never been one to cut out photos of wedding gowns or flower arrangements or wedding bands like some of her friends, so it wasn't loss of a big ceremony that would bother her, either.

So, what was bothering her the most? Why was she worried? She needed to discuss this more with Michael, so she finished dressing, stepped out of the room and discovered their suite was crowded with people decorating the patio, setting up tall candlesticks, tucking flowers here and there. So, they would be married right there in their room, she realized, amazed at the transformation of the space into something romantic.

Overwhelmed, she stayed rooted in place until Michael spotted her and came over.

"How can this happen?" she asked. "There are legal issues, time factors. It's late at night."

"No problem is too big if you're willing to pay the price. Apparently this happens often enough that the hotel has a contingency plan they can institute in min utes. You look beautiful, Felicity." He leaned around her, then handed her a bouquet of orchids, wild and exotic.

She didn't take them from him. "Did Sarah-Jane tell you I wanted to marry you?" He'd been sure of himself. Too sure, she realized. If he'd had the advantage of knowing that—

"Sarah-Jane did not tell me that."

She accepted the bouquet. Fifteen minutes later they were husband and wife. The ceremony wasn't entirely impersonal because the woman minister was warm and kind. The hotel staff serving as witnesses had gotten dressed up. A guitarist strummed and the trade winds blew. Still, it was a blur as Felicity repeated her vows, each one seeming more ominous than the last.

And yet Michael also promised to love, honor and cherish. No one held a gun to his head. His vows were made freely.

He loved her. He had to.

"I now pronounce you husband and wife. You may kiss your bride."

Until death do us part, Felicity thought as Michael's lips touched hers. She found contentment in the words, anxious finally to tell everyone at home.

But first there would be a wedding night to remember.

Married. After everyone left, Michael glanced at his wedding band, a matching one, although temporary, to Felicity's. He had a jeweler in Atlanta he trusted. He would buy her something there. In the meantime, they wore plain platinum bands.

Their meaning, however, was anything but plain. In fact it was all very complicated—except for the fact she was his now. Forever. She would be waiting for him at home every night. They would talk and laugh and make love. No more finding a date for events requiring his attendance. He could be open with her, trust her, not have to hold back for fear what he said might end up on Facebook or Twitter. Life would be good.

But for now, all he wanted was to make love to her.

He watched her standing on the patio, sipping champagne, a gentle breeze lifting her hair, so that it floated behind her. Her dress molded to her body. He knew what she looked like under it, would get to see that perfect body every day. Could shower with her, their soapy hands exploring each other. Could go to sleep and wake up spooned together.

Starting now.

He walked over to her, slipped her champagne flute out of her hand and set it aside. He lifted her in his arms and headed for the front door of their suite, where he opened it, walked through, turned around and carried her back inside. He wanted to do things right, make memories for her.

She smiled at him, not the sunny smile he'd come to know, but more passion-filled and seductive. She didn't have to hold back, and neither did he.

"Wait," she said. "I need to do something first. Be patient."

He set her down, and she took herself off to her bedroom. He poured himself a glass of champagne and downed it, trying not to speculate about what she was doing.

She emerged from her room in a diaphanous white negligee that hid and revealed at the same time. The fabric was sheer, but lace flowers provided modesty in places.

"You're beautiful," he said. He remembered a time when he hadn't thought so, only that she was fresh-faced and adorable, but now, to him, she was beautiful. How had he missed that?

She started to walk toward him, but he held up a hand. "Let me just look for a minute."

As she had with the bikini, she turned slowly, letting him admire her from all sides. There were no camouflaging flowers on the back side. He'd been aroused since he'd carried her across the threshold, the anticipation enough, but he'd reached breaking point.

She threw her arms wide, swirled once, then moved straight into his arms. In the bedroom he undressed himself in a hurry, then more slowly peeled her nightgown away. He'd seen her naked already, yet she looked different to him—and brand-new.

He cupped her head, looked into her brilliant blue eyes and saw love there. "This is going to make me sound pretty Neanderthal-like, Felicity, but I have to admit I'm happy to be your first. That you waited. I know it's old-fashioned—"

She put a hand over his mouth. "Then that makes me old-fashioned, too. Come. Love me."

She could have meant that two different ways, he

thought. Make love or just love. He wasn't sure he knew what love was, but he knew how to make love.

They started over, leaving what had happened behind, except he was more gentle with her, even when she begged him to hurry. He feasted on her mouth until she was panting, then moved to her breasts, enjoying the hardness of her nipples against his lips and tongue, while exploring her firm breasts that more than filled his hands. She grabbed his hair as he went lower, using his fingertips, breath and teeth to arouse her, sweeping her intimately with his tongue as gently as he could, holding her down as she arched up in response, making incredible, throaty sounds of pleasure, saying his name over and over. He let her almost peak, then backed off. She tried to pull him up to her, but he wanted to know she would be ready to take him inside, so he let her climax.

He hadn't heard anything so amazing in his life as the sounds that came from her. She made him feel more like a man than anyone ever had. And she was his woman now. Forever.

He settled on top of her, dug deep for control and entered her, aware of everything about her, every sound, every touch, every breath. He could feel her accommodate him, heard her making a soft sound of discomfort, then she rose to meet him. He didn't last any longer than she did, and it was powerful and endless and memorable. He collapsed against her, felt her wrap her arms and legs around him and hold tight.

After a minute he pulled away, feeling her shift under

him, surprised to see she was crying. "Did it hurt too much? I tried to be careful."

"Happy tears." Her smile was back, the one he knew. "I love you, Michael."

He kissed her, then held her close. They slept.

Chapter Eleven

Bright rays streamed through a skylight the next morning, bathing Felicity and Michael with warmth. She felt him curled behind her, asleep, his arm around her, as if he was afraid she would leave without his knowing.

It had been the most wonderful and complicated night of her life. He was a generous lover, and encouraged her to be generous with him as well. She may have been innocent, but she wasn't ignorant about sex and the various ways to experience it. She didn't just experience, she wallowed, she luxuriated, she gloried. She loved, and she'd said so.

But Michael hadn't. Every time she said the words, he kissed her, never saying anything.

In the light of day, doubt crowded her decision to marry him. Huge doubts. She realized she hadn't really been waiting for marriage to make love for the first time. She'd been waiting for love. And hadn't found it.

Until he came into her life, that is. But would it ever be returned?

And now she was married. What would happen next? Where would they live?

Her parents would be disappointed not to have been at her wedding. Would his? And all of his siblings and cousins? Sarah-Jane was going to be upset not to have been maid of honor. She already didn't like Michael. This would only seal the deal for her.

"Good morning, Mrs. Fortune," came a gravelly voice from behind her, his arm tightening, tugging her even closer. "How do you feel?"

"Kind of sore all over," she said honestly. "That was a workout."

"No gym membership required."

"What time do we need to check out?" she asked.

"In a couple hours, but I was thinking I might send Tanner home and have him come back in a few days. What do you think?"

She rolled over to face him. "I can't leave Liz to handle my shop without notice."

"Call and ask. I bet she says it's fine."

"After all we went through these past few days, she deserves time off, Michael, not more work. She's my aunt and my partner, not my employee."

He retreated at her tone, quickly transforming from lover to…to—

She didn't know what. Something more serious.

"All right," he said.

"We shouldn't put off telling everyone we got married, either. There'll be enough hurt feelings already."

He toyed with her hair. "I've been thinking maybe we keep it to ourselves for a while longer, let everyone get used to us as a couple before we spring it on them. Spin control in advance."

Felicity's lungs compressed. Her heart shrank. He was ashamed to tell people? "Are you sorry we got married?"

"I am not sorry at all."

His face was saying something different. His skin had gone pale, his eyes turned wary, his lips compressed. She climbed out of bed, got two robes from the bathroom and tossed him one before donning the other.

She sat on the bed, one leg tucked under her, her arms crossed. "Where are we going to live, Michael? Who's quitting their job?"

"That's something we'll work out."

He apparently hadn't given it a thought, which spoke volumes to her. It really was only about last night, about sleeping with her. Why in the world had he married her? She'd told him directly she would sleep with him, no marriage necessary.

What had she done?

"Do you love me, Michael?"

"I—"

"No crap, okay? Answer the question as honestly as you can. We made that promise to each other after the shrimp episode."

He put on the robe finally, taking his time, then he

sat on the bed, facing her. He took her hand. She tried to pull it back, but he held on.

"What's love?" he asked. "I don't know, Felicity. I hear about it, people sing about it, praise it, use it to destroy other people."

She refused to cry, but oh, those tears wanted to come.

"Here's what I know," he said. "I'll stay with you always. I will always be faithful to you. If we have children, I will be a better father than my father was. I will hold you in esteem, respect you, listen to you. But love? To me it's a myth. It's better to have a good friendship and passion. That's what we have. That's what lasts."

She couldn't believe her ears. She stood, wrapped her robe closer. Her blood ran cold. "That's not enough for me, Michael, so I'm not going to hold you to this marriage. More importantly, I don't want to be held to this marriage. I want forever, but I want to be loved as much as I love. We'll get an annulment. Heck, maybe the marriage isn't even legal."

She cinched the belt again until it hurt. "You should check into that. In fact, I expect you to take care of it, and soon."

Michael didn't move as she ran from the room. Annulled? No way. Wasn't going to happen. He went into the living room so that she couldn't leave without his knowing. A few minutes later she came out of her bedroom, her suitcase in hand. She pulled off her ring and handed it to him.

"I guess we have to share the plane for the trip back," she said. "But I'm done talking to you. Except to say this. Last night was lovely and romantic, and I will cherish it always."

He didn't try to stop her, didn't want to make things worse. The only thing that gave him hope was the catch in her voice. It mattered to her. It all mattered. For all that she was optimistic and light and fun, she wasn't flighty. If she hadn't wanted to marry him, she wouldn't have. Nothing he said or did would've mattered.

Michael took his time getting to the airport, not wanting to arrive too early. The terminal was small, so they couldn't avoid each other. It would be hard enough to share the plane for hours. He wouldn't try to convince her to change her mind on the plane. She was too fragile. He could do more harm than good at this point.

But he would court her again, win her back. She was his wife now.

Two hours later he arrived at the terminal. She was engaged in conversation with an attractive, well-dressed man with graying temples, and…presence, an air of authority. Michael hung back, watching, wondering, especially when she dug something out of her purse and passed it to him. Her business card, Michael figured, seeing the man give her one from his pocket, too. Some guy had come along, seen a damsel in distress and came riding over on his steed to rescue her.

Michael's world turned green with envy. She was smiling at the man, who laughed in return.

"All set?" Tanner came up beside Michael.

"Yeah."

After a few seconds, Tanner said, "Are you going to get Felicity?"

"Maybe you should." He turned and walked away, remembering where he needed to go to board the charter aircraft.

The copilot was already on board, so Michael went up the stairs and settled in his seat. Tanner and Felicity arrived a couple minutes later. Tanner stowed her luggage, then went to the cockpit without a word. She sat in the seat that had been a bed on the way down. They faced each other, but they weren't next to each other.

He wondered if she could last the whole trip without talking, but then she closed her eyes and went to sleep.

I don't want to be held to this marriage, she'd said.

Her rejection hurt. It hurt like nothing he'd ever experienced. And all because he couldn't say the three words she wanted? Maybe he should just do it. Say them. If it would set his world right again, what did it matter?

She woke up when they landed, grabbed her suitcase and went down the stairs as soon as they touched the tarmac.

"Do you need a ride home?" Tanner asked her.

"She'll ride with me," Michael said.

"Felicity?" Tanner's voice was gentle.

"It's fine. Thank you." She gave him a smile, picked up her bag and headed for the parking lot.

Michael caught up with her, matching strides. He put their luggage in the trunk. He'd no sooner gotten into the car than his phone rang. His sister Jordana. Tanner hadn't wasted any time reporting to his wife that there was trouble between Michael and Felicity.

Michael didn't answer it, nor later when his sister Emily called. After that one, he turned the phone off altogether.

"Do you want to be dropped off at home or the shop?" he asked.

"The shop, please."

He pulled around the back, where she could go in through the rear door and avoid being seen by the curious masses. No one needed to know she was there unless she chose to let them.

"Thank you for the ride," she said, polite to the end, as he set her suitcase at the door.

"Felicity—"

"Please don't," she said, looking at the ground.

"I have to go home for a couple of days. I had a message from my father when we landed. A problem with the buyout. But I'm coming back. I want to work things out with you. I'm not giving up."

"I can't tell you not to come back—you have a lot of family here, after all—but don't try to see me unless you've got annulment papers for me to sign. Goodbye, Michael."

She rolled her suitcase behind her into the shop. The door slammed in his face. As a farewell line, it'd been a good one. The problem was, Felicity didn't know that when someone told him he couldn't have or do something, it made him work harder for it. That was why he'd never failed to get what he wanted.

His winning streak wasn't about to end now. He *did* want to be held to his marriage.

Now all he needed was a plan.

* * *

"What did he do?" Sarah-Jane almost shouted as she flung open the back door of True Confections.

Felicity was trying not to show any emotion, not to her aunt, and now not to Sarah-Jane. "What did you hear? How did you hear?"

"You know this town. I got three phone calls in two minutes saying you and Michael weren't speaking, that he'd broken your heart."

Felicity forced herself to laugh. "That's ridiculous. Of course we're speaking. He drove me here. And why would everyone assume he broke my heart? Why don't you think I broke his?"

"Is that what happened?"

"Nothing in particular happened, Sarah-Jane. We just discovered that we weren't right for each other. It was just like you and Wyatt said. We're opposites. We attracted, then we found nothing important in common." She washed her hands, wanting to do something, make something. "Who's holding down the store?"

"I put up the Gone Fishin' sign," Sarah-Jane said. "People will wait or come back." She moved closer to Felicity, made her look at her. "You're in pain."

Felicity rolled her eyes. "I am not. I had a good time actually. I swam in the Caribbean Sea. I had a lovely dinner as the sun set. He got a two-bedroom suite, so I had my own room. It was fine."

"Fine." Sarah-Jane tossed her head. "Fine," she muttered again as she walked out the door.

"So, how did we end up for Valentine's Day?" Felicity asked her aunt brightly.

"I ran a total for you, kept it in my pocket in case you called and asked." She passed it to her niece, her gaze steady. "Not only that, but business continues to come online. And others have called to say their friend/mother/whoever said they were given some of your truffles for Valentine's Day and they had to try them."

"Wow." Felicity stared at the numbers. "That's amazing."

"You paid for a lot of help, too, of course, so your expenses are higher, but you made a tidy sum. If you keep this up, you could buy that little house you want a lot sooner than you expected."

"I met a gentleman at the airport who plans conventions all over the world. He wants to talk long-term contract with me." She put a hand against her stomach for a second. "It's happening."

"If you want it. You're not deep enough into it at this point that you couldn't go back to the way things were."

Felicity nodded. "Lots to think about. Why don't you go home, Liz? I caught up on my sleep. You must be exhausted." She hugged her aunt. "I couldn't have done this without you. No way."

"I had a whole lot of fun, you know. You've built a business that isn't anything like mine was when you took it over. I wish I'd had your talent and determination. I'm so proud of you."

Liz left and the kitchen was empty and quiet. Felicity pulled out some bittersweet chocolate and heavy cream. She'd had in mind a new truffle ever since she'd gone to the Sweets Market with Michael. Without thinking about it, she'd just pulled out the chocolate he'd loved best. Next she reached for a bottle of amaretto liqueur.

When she was done making the small, experimental batch, she topped each one with an almond, then drizzled a chocolate heart over it.

Felicity sat back and stared at what she'd created. She'd planned all along to make it for him, with the flavors that had appealed to him, even down to the heart on top. She was going to call it the Fortune Truffle and surprise him with it the next time he came to town.

She took a bite, closed her eyes and let it melt in her mouth. Only then did the tears start to flow. She laid her head on the table and let them fall, mourning the loss of him, missing him like a piece of herself. He'd been worth the wait—until he wasn't.

After a while, she got up, dumped the candy in the trash and vowed never to make them again.

That chapter of her life was closed for good.

"Crisis averted." John Michael poured himself and his son a bourbon on the rocks. "Good job, son."

"Thanks." Michael had turned off his emotions as he'd dealt with the new financial demands Trexler had made, but now they crept back. He was cold inside. Ice-cold. He'd gone from the highest high of his life to the lowest low in the blink of an eye.

He didn't want to be here, but he sipped his drink from the chair across the desk from his father, who suddenly decided instead of sitting behind his desk, to take a seat in the visitor chair next to Michael.

Michael hid his surprise. His father always kept his

desk between them, establishing a barrier between boss and employee, if not father and son.

"I've been giving some thought to our conversation the other day," John Michael said. "You seemed to be contemplating creating a business of your own, which means you'd leave the company."

Michael didn't acknowledge the statement. He hadn't said that to his father, but to his mother, so she'd obviously told. John Michael smiled a little, raised his glass, then went on.

"I can understand your being frustrated in your position, knowing it's a long time until you completely assume command, but I see you need to take on a more active role."

"One with autonomy," Michael said. "I've proven I have vision. I've proven I make good decisions."

"You have. So, here's what I'm proposing. I'll add president and creative director to your title. I'll remain CEO, but my role will change. I have strengths in different areas from you. I'll focus on keeping current customers happy. I know how the good ol' boys' network works. You can do what you've been asking to for years—use the new technologies to expand our business in whatever way you think will work. It'll almost be like creating your own company. What do you think?"

He was granting Michael the wish highest on his career list, one he'd hungered for. And yet…he'd been giving a lot of thought to starting from scratch himself, building from the ground up. Maybe in San Antonio, which was close enough to have a house in Red Rock.

He wasn't cut out for ranching like his cousins, but that didn't mean he couldn't live in ranch country.

Plus he had the incentive of his wife already living there and probably not wanting to move. His wife may have other ideas, like ordering him to end the marriage, but that was not an option to Michael.

"I appreciate the offer, Dad. I need to give it some thought."

John Michael had let down his guard, so Michael saw the surprise and disappointment in his father's eyes. "So, the young miss from Red Rock has spun a sugar web around you."

"That's part of it."

A short knock on the door preceded his mother sweeping into the room, dressed to the nines, as she liked to say.

"Hello, darlings," she said, as both men rose. She gave Michael a hug, then sat in the chair that John Michael vacated, while he returned to the one behind his desk.

"You look beautiful, Mom."

"Thank you. Your father is taking me to dinner at Aria." She gave her husband a loving look, something Michael had never seen before. Had she always looked at him like that?

He glanced quickly at his father, whose expression remained the same, not bored, exactly, but definitely not openly loving. Was that how he and Felicity would appear to other people? One aloof and one adoring? Wouldn't people feel sorry for Felicity? Because he had to admit, he felt sorry for his mother.

"Your father and I would like to meet Felicity, Michael. Could you arrange that now that her Valentine's Day rush is over? We understand that her shop is closed on Sunday and Monday, so perhaps she could fly here Saturday night and come to Sunday brunch with the family. Emily and Max will be in town. Blake and Katie said they could make it."

"Probably not this weekend, Mom. Maybe another time."

"Trouble in paradise?" his father asked.

"Nothing I can't handle." He caught his father's gaze. "Your scheme worked, by the way. Her business went wild."

"Did it make her happy?"

"I think she has mixed feelings about it. I think it was too much too soon. She's smart, and if she'd grown the business exponentially, she would be more comfortable. Having it crash around her wasn't fair. You had to know—because you're an astute businessman yourself—that setting her up that way wasn't a good idea."

"Do you think I was trying to sabotage her? Why would I do that? I don't know the woman. I do know you. You would need a strong partner. It sounds like she survived just fine."

"So you were auditioning her for me?"

John Michael ran a hand down his face. "I thought I was doing her a favor, giving her exposure. You know, son, just because someone does something nice for you doesn't mean they're out to get you. I wasn't killing her with kindness."

Michael didn't know what to believe. He'd personally seen his father manipulate people and situations. Maybe he'd never know.

"I think this conversation has gone on long enough, Michael," his mother said.

There was much more he wanted to say and to ask. Instead, he stood, offered his father a handshake and a silent message that he would get back to him. He hugged his mother then, taking comfort in her familiar perfume and the peace that came with it. "Enjoy your dinner."

He would go work out at the gym, where he got a lot of thinking done. He would come up with a plan, not just to win Felicity back but for the rest of his life.

Then he would implement the plan and his world would settle down again instead of being topsy-turvy and at odds. He didn't function well in those conditions.

His life had been unpredictable since the moment he met Felicity.

It was time to stop the craziness.

Chapter Twelve

"I don't care what words come out of your mouth," Sarah-Jane said to Felicity Sunday morning, the only day they had off together. "Your eyes say something different. They say you're sad."

Sarah-Jane was headed to a barbecue with Wyatt later, but for the moment, the roommates could relax over breakfast at home for the first time in weeks.

"Those are tired eyes, my friend," Felicity said. "After one more full night's sleep, I'll be good as new, I promise. I'm going to help Liz today. It's hard for her to clean house on crutches. And I owe her big time."

"I don't know why you won't tell me what happened with Michael, because I know something did. Wyatt is furious, too."

"You should both relax. I have." Felicity got up from the table and took their dishes to the sink, the kitchen a mess from fixing omelets, bacon and country-fried potatoes. It was the first full meal she'd been able to stomach. At least she hadn't cried herself to sleep last night. That was progress, too.

Together they cleaned up the dishes and made a potato salad for Sarah-Jane to take with her. Sarah-Jane had done Felicity's share of the housework, even her laundry, during the past couple of weeks, so she could just enjoy the day.

The morning was beautiful as she headed to Liz's house. She made her way down Main Street, looking in the store windows.

When she reached the diner, Estelle spotted her and held up a finger for her to wait. Sighing, Felicity stopped.

"You hungry?" Estelle asked as she joined Felicity outside.

"Just ate, thanks."

"You okay, honey? I heard what happened."

Felicity spread her arms and looked up. "Exactly what did you hear?" No one could possibly know the truth, because she hadn't told anyone. Guesswork and speculation, the root of all gossip.

"That the Suit broke your heart."

"Well, you heard wrong. And why is it that no one thinks I broke his?" she asked, not for the first time and probably not the last. "Don't you think I'm capable of that?"

"Of course we do, honey. But we all know you're in love with the man, even though he doesn't deserve it. How can anyone break the heart of an iceman?"

Felicity blew out a breath. She should just give up. They all loved her too much, which she shouldn't complain about. "I'm good, Estelle. I'm great, in fact. Thank you for your concern."

She walked away, only to get stopped again outside Break Time when one of the baristas ran to catch her. "I just tried to call you. Come inside, Felicity. You need to see this."

The young woman pointed to the candy case, which was completely empty. "We restocked from what was in the back, but it's all gone. What should we do?"

The diligent, responsible Felicity felt a need to get to work, to fill the case again, especially if people were driving from any distance to buy her wares.

But her inner champion talked her out of it, citing potential mental instability—or worse—if she gave in to her instincts.

"Please tell the customers we're terribly sorry. That the demand was beyond our expectations, but we'll have plenty available when we open again on Tuesday."

She'd never been without stock before. If Liz couldn't help her tomorrow, Felicity would have to hire someone. In fact, she should do that anyway, at least to wash bowls and utensils and be their gofer. Another trip to the Sweets Market would be necessary this week, too.

Hiring and firing. She really didn't want to do that. She could plan for the holidays, but she hadn't counted on this bonanza.

She kept walking, trying to forget about the problem for now, trying to empty her mind of everything work— or Michael—related. She found Liz on her front porch, enjoying the morning, her foot with the cast resting on an ottoman, a teapot and a plate with two cranberry scones on a small table within reach.

"Good morning, sweetheart. Come sit with me. Scone?"

"I couldn't eat a bite, thanks." She sat on the padded seat next to her aunt. "There's not enough white space open on your cast for one more autograph and get-well-soon message."

"I'm a lucky girl, aren't I? All these wonderful friends and neighbors. And you." She patted Felicity's thigh. "I appreciate your offering to clean my house, but I can afford to have someone in, you know."

It was the right opening for a question that had been on Felicity's mind for years. "How is that, Liz? I know you never made enough money at the candy business to provide a real income for yourself. How do you afford your life? You don't have to answer, of course, but—"

Liz interrupted her with a gesture. "I'll tell you. It's no great secret, just no one else's business really."

"I know you came to Red Rock because of a man."

"In a way. I was your age and had been working out of Dallas as a flight attendant. I loved my job. I hadn't been doing it long enough to be jaded, I suppose," she said with a shrug. "I met Ethan on a flight from Boston to Dallas, and was smitten, as smitten as you were with Michael that first day." She smiled sympathetically.

"This is about you, Auntie."

"Don't call me that. It makes me feel old," she said, an ongoing joke between them. "Anyway, the flight was delayed because of weather, and the passengers weren't allowed to deplane. He was in first class. In those days there weren't as many people seated there because the frequent-flyer program hadn't been created. Ethan was the only first-class passenger, so we ended up talking a lot."

"What did he look like?"

"An everyday Greek god. Tall, fit, curly dark hair, strong features, but with a kind soul. And a wedding ring. We said goodbye at the end of the trip, didn't exchange phone numbers. I thought that was the end of it. But a couple of weeks later, he called. We met for dinner. I knew I shouldn't go, but I couldn't help myself."

Felicity understood that irrational pull, the thing that made you do something you knew you shouldn't. She was married now because of it.

"His wife was bedridden, had been for years, a quadriplegic from a sports accident the fifth year they were married. They had two young sons. He took good care of her, Felicity. He never once considered abandoning her. But she'd seen something different in him after we met and questioned him about it. When he admitted to being attracted, she encouraged him to contact me, that she understood he had needs."

"Wow, there's an understanding and brave woman."

"She trusted his love, knew he would stay. He said no. So she got someone to track me down, ran a full background check and decided she approved. Ethan and I didn't sleep together. We met for dinner, we danced, we talked, we held each other. Oh, I was so in love with him. So desperately in love. I would've done anything for him. He never asked. But then as thcsc thing happen, I finally realized I couldn't do it anymore. I wanted a life with him, normalcy, and he could never give that to me. He didn't try to stop me, said he didn't have the right to ask."

Liz took a sip of her tea, her eyes distant but not sad. "I didn't see him for a year, then I saw his wife's obituary in the newspaper. I wanted to run to him, but I waited instead. His boys were twelve and ten by then. They needed Ethan more than ever. It took four months for him to come to me. I welcomed him, made love with him and loved him until the day he told me he was getting married, six months later."

Felicity gasped. "What a jerk! How could he do that to you after all you'd gone through for him?"

"Shh. I know it sounds horrible, and it was at the time. But, sweetheart, I couldn't and don't blame him. I allowed it to happen. I was the one in love, not him. He needed me. I came into his life at the exact moment he needed someone to lean on, and I provided that. But he never loved me, never said the words, never saw me as a potential mother to his sons. To him I was a flighty flight attendant who'd had an affair with someone I'd met on a plane. I don't think he trusted that I wasn't doing that—or worse—on a regular basis."

"He knew you all those years and he didn't trust you?"

"Apparently. Anyway, he was a very wealthy man, and he wanted to make sure I wouldn't cause complications with his new bride, so he offered to buy me a house anywhere I wanted."

"You took him up on that?" Felicity pressed a hand to her chest.

"No." Liz smiled. "Got you for a minute, though, didn't I?"

"Well, it didn't sound like the Liz I know and love."

"I sent him on his way, but the seed had been planted about living somewhere else. I'd saved quite a bit of money, but it wasn't enough to retire so early, then I got an inheritance from my parents' estate. Your father did, too, remember?"

"Yes. It helped pay for college tuitions and weddings."

"Well, mine bought me this house in this pretty little town and a perfectly adequate annuity."

"Why have I been thinking he was the love of your life?"

"You got that romantic notion in your head, and I never told you otherwise. I met other men, dated a lot, but never fell in love again."

"Men fell in love with you. I met a couple of them."

"Sometimes it takes only one experience to ruin you for life. All in all, I've been happy being independent."

Felicity studied her aunt. Was she happy? It had to be possible to get past an experience like she had with Ethan. Men weren't all alike. But who was she, Felicity Thomas, neophyte at love, to question her aunt? And maybe Liz's memory wasn't perfect. Maybe she hadn't been willing to bend for Ethan, and he got tired of waiting.

Felicity had gotten into an untenable position herself.

Maybe she'd been too much of a mule. There were two sides to every story, after all.

"You know, Auntie, you could've just told me from the beginning that you inherited the money."

"There was no lesson in that, though, was there?"

Felicity clenched her hands in her lap, not wanting to hear what came next, but knowing she had to. "Meaning?"

"Ethan never loved me. I was a convenience, then a detriment. It was good that we broke up."

"So, you're saying it was good that Michael and I broke up?"

"When did you become so dense?" She sighed. "I don't know what happened to you and Michael while you were gone, but I know you love each other. Here's a truth, sweetheart. We can waste time being with someone we'll never end up with, like I did—or we can waste time fighting being with someone we should end up with, like you are. Don't waste time."

Felicity looked away, feeling as barren as the surrounding trees still waiting for spring. "He doesn't love me," she said quietly.

"Of course he does."

"He says he doesn't. He doesn't believe in love."

"Oh. Well, that's a different thing altogether." Liz frowned. "I'm not sure how to advise you, then. You were right to cut your losses. He's a fool."

Maybe so, but he was *her* fool. And it was one thing for Felicity to think that herself, and another for her aunt to say it out loud. "He wants me back," she said, defensive.

"You can do better."

Felicity wasn't sure if her aunt was being serious or pulling her leg, if Liz's own experience was coloring her view or she was goading Felicity into action. "I wish I knew what to do."

A shiny black sports car drove by, the kind Michael always rented. A few seconds later it was backing up the street, then stopped in front of Liz's house. Felicity clenched the arm rest. She touched her hair, remembering she'd just pulled it up with a barrette, expecting to be cleaning house.

"He's wearing Wranglers," she said, watching him stride up the walkway, a bouquet of daisies in his hand. "And a cowboy shirt."

"With creases sharp enough to cut paper," Liz added. "Let's hope he didn't buy pointy-toed boots."

He came to a stop on the top stair, rested a booted foot—with a just-right toe—on the porch itself.

"Mornin', Felicity. Liz."

He wasn't wearing a Stetson, but he sure sounded like a cowboy. The ice around Felicity's heart thawed a little at the effort he was making.

"Hey, there, cowpoke," Liz said, grabbing her crutches and standing. "I have something important to do. Like watch my dust bunnies grow."

After she went into the house, Michael stepped onto the porch. He sat next to Felicity, but their shoulders brushed once, briefly, and she hopped up and moved away.

"These are for you," he said, leaning forward far

enough to hand her the bouquet. "I sent you roses before I really knew you. These suit you better."

She did what any woman would, she pressed her face into them, then she didn't know what to do. She couldn't just hold on to them.

He stood, came close, raised a hand toward her face. She yanked back. "Don't."

"You've got pollen from the flowers," he said, brushing at it, then dropping his hand and stepping back. "We need to talk."

"Not here," she whispered harshly, her heart thundering. He looked so handsome in his Western clothes, casual and huggable. "She'll hear everything through that window behind you."

"All right. Let's go for a drive."

"Let's walk up the road a bit." She opened Liz's front door and set her flowers inside first. "Okay."

"How have you been?" Michael asked, matching his strides to hers. He wanted—needed—to hold her hand. He'd missed her, felt empty without her. For a while he'd carried around one of her mints, but it melted in his pocket. He'd been devastated by it, which came as more of a shock to him than anything else that had happened. It was just a piece of candy, but…

"Did you bring the annulment papers?" she asked.

"Even I can't accomplish that so quickly."

"I told you not to come back unless you have them."

"And I said I wasn't giving up."

She veered off the road and down a well-trod path. He didn't know where it led, but then he heard water, a nearby stream.

"I don't think we'll be overheard here," she said, stopping and crossing her arms.

It wasn't a particularly scenic spot. The stream wasn't running fast and the bushes were scraggly, but she was there, and that was all that mattered.

"The only reason I'm talking to you," she said, "is to tell you what everyone here thinks, and what I've told people, so we're on the same page. Obviously, I didn't tell anyone about the wedding, so no one will know about that. Everyone has jumped to the conclusion that you broke my heart, so they pretty much—"

"Hate me?"

She shrugged. "I tried at every opportunity to say they got it wrong, that I broke *your* heart, but no one believes me. I shared a little more with Liz, but that's all."

"Not Sarah-Jane?"

"She's marrying into your family. Knowing her, she'd hold it against you and you'd be banned from all the family events she'll ever host down the road."

He didn't think Wyatt would allow that, but he held his tongue. "So, you're saying I have an uphill battle not only with you but with the entire town."

"You have no battle with me. As for the town, does it matter to you?"

He was surprised how much it mattered. He wanted to be accepted here, where everyone loved and protected her. He didn't want to be a pariah. "It matters, Felicity. I have family here. They're sticking."

"Then I don't know what to say. It won't be easy. I'm sorry about that. I've tried to put the blame on myself, but no one's buying it. It's been really hard."

"Not much about this relationship has been easy."

Her lips compressed into a straight, hard line. Her eyes narrowed. "Well, gee, Mr. Bigwig Fortune, who always gets what he wants. I'm so sorry I haven't just buckled under and done everything you asked all the time. Haven't fawned at your feet. Haven't waited by the phone for you to call." She moved in on him. "I'm entitled to my feelings. I'm entitled to love and *be loved*. I'll find it, that much I guarantee you."

"I didn't mean it like you're taking it. Felicity." He reached for her as she turned away and took off. He caught up in a hurry. "I like that it hasn't been easy, that you've challenged me. That you wouldn't let me run the relationship. I've been learning to compromise. All I'm asking is that you compromise with me on this issue between us."

She stopped in her tracks. "You think this is an *issue?* This is my *life*."

"And mine." He pounded his chest. "Ours. I married you because I wanted to. I want to stay married. I need you to give me—us—a chance."

She didn't say anything, which he took as a good thing.

"Let's start over," he said. He wanted to touch her, but he was pretty sure she would rebuff him. "We can spend time together. Learn more about each other. Do things differently. You've always struck me as a fair person, one who gives second chances. Before you turn your back completely, will you give us one more try?"

Felicity stared at the ground as his words settled over her. He was right. She wasn't one to give up—unless she saw no hope. Was there no hope? She'd made a vow. But so had he, and his was a lie. He promised to love. He didn't.

"Have dinner with me tonight. Pretend it's our first date," he said.

She felt him stroke her hair. Intending to clean house, she hadn't even showered yet. She felt grungy. "Don't," she said, pulling away.

He didn't say anything, but she knew he was upset just by the way he stood.

"Okay," she said, and watched a transformation come over him. Not overt happiness, but relief probably. She finally realized how tired he looked, as if he hadn't been sleeping. Or maybe he'd been sick. She didn't want to care so much, but— "Are you all right?" she asked, searching the dark depths of his eyes.

"I'm getting better. Can we start now?"

"Start?"

"The date."

She touched her hair self-consciously again. "I told Liz I'd help clean her house today."

"I'll help. Then we'll go."

She tried not to laugh. He was being so un-Michael like. He wasn't smooth and in charge, but visibly eager. "I'll need to shower and change."

"No problem."

They walked back to Liz's house. She wanted to hold his hand like they usually did. And as long as she was being honest with herself, she wanted their date to be at his hotel room, in bed. Maybe her emotions were in turmoil, but her body knew him now, knew the pleasure and satisfaction he gave. Knew how pleasurable it was to make love to him, too, openly, without hesitation, with gusto.

"I've missed you, Felicity."

She almost broke down. Tears filled her eyes and burned her throat, but she wouldn't say the words back to him, even though they were true for her, too.

Why was love so complicated?

Chapter Thirteen

Sarah-Jane didn't hide her annoyance when she and Wyatt came into the apartment hours later. "What are *you* doing here?"

"Hello to you, too," Michael said. "Wyatt."

"Felicity let you in?" Sarah-Jane asked. "Where is she?"

"Getting ready for our date." He knew their response represented the town as a whole. He'd decided not to use words but actions to gain their approval.

"I suppose you brought her those daisies." She sniffed. "At least you got that right this time."

He almost smiled. "Thank you."

She raced upstairs, leaving Michael alone with Wyatt.

"Is it true?" Wyatt asked.

Michael braced himself. "What?"

"Felicity says she's the one who ended things, yet here you are, taking her out."

"There's blame to share, Wyatt. We decided we'd invested a lot and we weren't ready to give up."

Wyatt threw up his hands. "You are so like your father. She isn't a business, Mike. You don't *invest* in her. You treat her well. You love her. Or you get the hell out."

Michael clenched his teeth. "How hard would you work to keep Sarah-Jane if she decided right now not to marry you?"

"Hard," Wyatt said, the word coming out rough. "With everything I've got."

"Well, that's what I'm doing. And just for the record, Wyatt, you don't like being compared to your father, either. Who knows? Maybe we're *all* like our parents, whether we like it or not. But one thing we all seem to have in common is that we don't give up."

Wyatt conceded the point with a small gesture. "It's just that I hear it all from Sarah-Jane, and she's prejudiced toward Felicity, of course."

"It shouldn't be any other way. It says a lot about Felicity that she has such great, supportive friends." He realized he didn't. Maybe that was why it mattered so much that he not lose the respect and affection of his siblings and cousins. They'd been the ones who'd mattered all these years. Would continue to matter.

Sarah-Jane came down the stairs, Felicity right behind her. Even though her hair was still damp from her shower, she'd never looked more beautiful to him, quite literally took his breath away. He rubbed his chest where his heart had seemed to expand too quickly as she came up beside him. She wasn't even dressed up, but had on jeans and one of her lacy tops.

Michael had to look away from her, was suddenly worried about spending an evening with her without touching. He turned to Wyatt. "We're going bowling. You two want to come along?"

"Bowling? Really?" Felicity said, then made eye contact with Sarah-Jane. They both smiled.

"*I'd* like to," Sarah-Jane said. She turned to Wyatt and gave him a you'd-better-agree look that even Michael could read.

"Fine with me," Wyatt said.

Felicity picked up her purse from the kitchen table. "What made you choose bowling, Michael?"

If he were being honest with her, he'd tell her he wanted to be able to sit and watch her, especially from behind. He was smarter than that, however. "It seemed like something fun to do. And different."

"Hmm. Okay."

They all moved toward the front door, but Felicity stopped at the coat closet and pulled out a jacket for Sarah-Jane, then one for herself. Then she crouched and dug deep in the closet, coming out with a bowling ball bag.

"You have your own ball?" Michael asked as Wyatt and Sarah-Jane left the apartment.

"If you'd accepted my invitation to see my bedroom that time I asked, you would've seen my bowling trophies. Not all of them because they wouldn't all fit, and it would look tacky." She grinned at him, then let him precede her so that she could lock the front door.

Her smile seemed normal and easy, which validated his choice of activity for their date. He hadn't been sure he would ever see that again.

Plus there was the bonus of watching her rear end constantly and no one could accuse him of crossing an invisible line of public good taste.

It was a good start.

Felicity loved bowling alley sounds, the crash of the pins, the whoops and hollers and groans. And the food. Best ever. She'd been in a league from the time she was eight until she was eighteen, and had eaten more bowling alley food than home-cooked a lot of that time. For her it was like going home.

"I'll bet you've never had a chili dog before," Felicity said to Michael as Sarah-Jane stood poised to take her turn. Wyatt took it upon himself to curve his body behind hers, showing her how to swing. Never mind that they were in the last frame of their second game and Sarah-Jane had scored more points than Wyatt....

"I'm not a complete snob," Michael countered. He was leaning back, his arms stretched out along the top of the seat. his fingertips almost touching her shoulder. "I go to Super Bowl parties. And baseball games."

Felicity had fallen in love with him all over again. He'd shown her a side she hadn't seen, interacting with others, even players on other lanes. He did know how to have fun without spending a lot of money, without a whole lot of planning.

She wanted to sit on his lap and loop her arm around his neck, as Sarah-Jane had done a few times with

Wyatt. Every time it'd been her turn, Felicity could feel Michael's gaze follow her every move, a kind of foreplay she hadn't experienced before. To be that wanted was new.

"Hey, Champ, you're up," Michael said.

She didn't know how it happened. She took her usual four steps, then her feet went out from under her—

"Felicity!" Michael was bending over her, his face upside down to her, but a frantic expression there. Sarah-Jane leaned over his shoulder, wringing her hands.

She tried to stand, but no one would let her. "What happened?"

"You slipped in some water, maybe a melting ice cube. Your feet went out from under you and you fell," Michael said, taking hold of her hand. "You were unconscious. Scared us all. Sarah-Jane, you have her purse?"

"Got it."

"Why?" Felicity asked.

"We're going to the E.R."

"I'm fine."

"You were unconscious."

"For how long?"

"I don't know. It seemed like an hour."

"Seventy-two seconds," Wyatt said.

They all looked at him. "Advanced first aid in high school," he told them with a shrug. "Where I also learned that head injuries are nothing to mess with."

"There, you see?" Michael said to her. "I'll help you up."

She sat with help, felt a little light-headed. "Can't I just go home and see my own doctor?"

"It's Sunday, sweetie," Sarah-Jane said. "Besides, she'd just send you to the hospital anyway."

"I can't go there." She pushed away everyone's hands, then grabbed her head. Suddenly she was being eased to the ground again. A few strangers were hanging around at the fringes of their lane, employees, she guessed. She hated being on display like that.

"I can't afford a hospital stay," she whispered to Michael. "I don't have health insurance."

She and Sarah-Jane both had decided to risk going without for a while. The premiums had risen so much, it was a choice of paying for insurance or eating. They chose to eat.

"I'll cover it," Michael said. "Don't worry about it."

"You're not paying for my bill," she said, not really feeling up to doing battle with him, but making a token effort for the moment.

"Yes, I am."

"No."

"Yes."

"No, Michael, you're not."

"Okay. Technically I'm not. You're on my health insurance plan."

"Why would you do that?" Sarah-Jane asked. "How is it even possible? She would have to be your—" She stopped, put a hand over her mouth, then stared at Felicity, her eyes wide.

After a few seconds, Michael finished her sentence. "Wife."

Felicity groaned. Michael figured the sound of frustration had more to do with what he'd just admitted than how she felt.

He and Wyatt helped her to her feet, then Michael carried her. As soon as they were all settled in the car and Wyatt was driving to the hospital, Felicity said to the car in general, "Please don't tell anyone."

"I don't understand. When did you get married?" Sarah-Jane asked, turning around.

"Valentine's Day. Night."

"You didn't tell me." Hurt shaded her eyes. "I'm your best friend."

Michael took Felicity's hand. "It was a spontaneous thing."

"Obviously. Because you were a virgin?" Sarah-Jane asked. "You wouldn't sleep with him unless he married you?"

"It was kinda the other way around," Felicity said, putting Michael on the spot. "He wouldn't, unless—"

"That's enough," Michael said. No one needed to know their business, even if it was to protect his reputation. He could take it.

"No, it's not enough, Michael Fortune," Sarah-Jane said. "You swoop into town, sweep her off her feet, *marry* her and now you have her lying, too. Felicity Thomas, who never told a lie."

"That's not true," Felicity said. "I've lied."

"About what? That you only floss six nights a week

when you tell your dentist it's every night? Everyone lies to dentists."

"I floss every night," Felicity said weakly.

"Oh, for heaven's sake. I was just making something up. My point being, if you lie, it's not about anything important or so that someone else doesn't get hurt. Getting married is rather important, don't you think? Important enough to tell your friends and family. Unless you're ashamed of what you did."

"Calm down," Wyatt said. "Let them explain."

Michael had had enough. "We don't have to explain. And Sarah-Jane, now is not the time. Felicity's hurting enough as it is."

Sarah-Jane turned around in a huff. "I knew you were trouble the first moment I saw you."

"It takes two," Felicity said quietly, her eyes shut. "He doesn't get all the blame. I'm sorry you're feeling hurt and left out, Sarah-Jane."

They pulled up to the E.R. entrance. Michael wouldn't leave Felicity's side, so Sarah-Jane went in and got someone with a wheelchair. They sat in the waiting room, none of them speaking.

When the doctor examined Felicity, she yelped when he touched the back of her head. "You've got a doozy of a knot," he said. "I'm not seeing any confusion, no nausea. We can do a CT scan just to make sure there's no bleeding in the brain, but I'm betting it's only under the scalp."

"I'm good with that," Felicity said.

"She'll have the CT scan," Michael said. No one said no when he used that tone of voice, and this time didn't prove any different. The doctor didn't even glance at Felicity.

When the scan proved negative, they headed for home with the instructions to be cautious, take ibuprofen only for the pain and to be awakened a couple of times during the night.

The drive back to Red Rock was made in silence. It wasn't until they were inside the apartment that Michael announced, "I'll be staying here tonight."

No one challenged him.

"I just want to know one thing," Sarah-Jane said to Felicity, ignoring Michael. "Why didn't you tell me? All of us?"

"Because we decided to end it the next morning."

"More precisely, *she* decided," Michael said.

"Not good enough in bed for you?" Wyatt asked Felicity, making her laugh, then a moment later, grab the back of her head and groan.

Michael knew his cousin had just been relieving the tension in the room. It was a good time to part company. He tossed his rental car keys to Wyatt. "I haven't checked into the hotel, so my bag's in the car. If you wouldn't mind getting it, then putting it outside Felicity's door?"

"Sure."

Michael picked her up and headed for the staircase.

"I can walk, Michael."

"Probably so, but you're not going to. Good night, Sarah-Jane."

"I can relieve you. We can take shifts," she said.

"Not necessary, thanks." *She's mine to watch over. Mine to protect. Mine.*

"Which room?" he asked, then went where Felicity pointed.

He was wrong. It wasn't like walking into pink cotton candy, as he'd predicted. It was…nice. Girly, but nice. No frills, and no pink at all. The color reminded him of her shop, even her truck. Aqua, she'd called it, but balanced with ivories and beiges. A soothing space, he thought. Three large trophies shaped like bowling pins sat on a shelf, with other mementos scattered about—photos of her family, posters of Italy and Spain. A framed picture of him making cotton candy rested on her vanity, a single dried red rose lay in front of it.

She hadn't let go of him completely.…

"Welcome to my world," she said.

"You have a picture of me." He let her down next to the double bed so that he could fold back the aqua-and-yellow bedspread.

"A memento of a good day. Your sister Wendy took it and emailed it to me."

"Why aren't you fighting me about staying with you tonight?" he asked.

"Would it do me any good?"

"No."

"Well, then. Talking makes my head hurt. Arguing would be excruciating. I just want to sleep."

"You know I have to wake you every couple hours."

"I heard what the doctor said." She perched on the bed. "My nightgowns are hanging in the far right of my closet. Would you mind getting one?"

He saw the white negligee she'd worn on their wedding night first, touching it as he reached for the blue cotton one behind it, memories slamming into him of that night. That glorious night.

Followed by that horrible morning.

He crouched beside her to pull off her boots, then took off her socks, which had red balloons printed all over them.

"I can do the rest, thank you," she said, grabbing the gown and heading to her en suite bathroom.

After she shut the door, he collapsed on the bed, shaking, his head in his hands. The hideous sound of her head hitting the wood floor stuck with him. What if she'd died? He'd heard of that happening from a hard fall. When she didn't come to right away, he almost went crazy as he knelt on the floor beside her, holding her hand, willing her to open her eyes.

Trying to settle himself, Michael ran his hands through his hair and blew out a breath. He could hear the buzz of her electric toothbrush. When it finally stopped, he picked himself up off the bed, and tried to look calm, as though the accident hadn't shaken him. He told himself he would be okay for the rest of the night. He had to be strong for her.

A few seconds later, the door handle turned. He didn't want her to see him in the aftermath of his meltdown, so he went to the bedroom door and grabbed his suitcase from the hall. She climbed into bed and closed her eyes.

He took his turn in the bathroom, then pulled off his boots before he dragged a little upholstered chair close to the bed. He set alerts on his cell phone to wake him in case he fell asleep, but he didn't see that happening. He reached over to turn out her lamp.

She opened her eyes and looked right at him.

"Do you need something for the pain?" he asked.

"I'm okay for now. Are you planning to sit in that chair all night?"

"It's the only one around." It was ridiculously uncomfortable, too. He couldn't even lean back.

She levered herself up on her elbow. "Don't be stupid. There's half a bed here not being used."

"I'll be fine."

"Oh, quit being such a Fortune."

"Exactly what does that mean?"

"It means you're human. You need sleep, too, superhero. You've set your alerts. That'll be enough, don't you think?"

Michael slid down in the chair, stretched out his legs and crossed his ankles. "What's the best gift you've ever gotten?" he asked.

"Christmas, birthday or for no reason?"

He smiled and shook his head. "One of each."

"Christmas when I was four—a bald preemie Cabbage Patch doll named Herbie. I carried it everywhere for a year. My fifteenth birthday—a push-up bra my sister Lila gave me. We giggled about it for days. And for no reason? A dozen red roses from you, because they made me feel pretty. How about you?"

"Your virginity."

He got out of the chair and crouched beside the bed. He saw in her eyes how much his answer had affected her. "I could sleep in the half of your bed that's not being used, but in some ways it would be more uncomfortable than that chair."

"I won't do battle about it, Michael. I just want you to have as easy a night as possible." She brushed her fingers across his cheek. "I know if the situation was reversed, I would be doing the same as you. And that you would talk me out of it."

"A compromise of sorts, then," he said. He got into bed and sat with his back against the headboard, keeping his clothes on and not getting under the covers.

After a minute, she shifted closer to him, until her forehead touched his hip. He tried to think about anything other than how close her lips were to his skin, only a layer of denim away. As it was, he could feel her breath, warm and steady through the fabric.

Oh, what the hell, he thought, giving in, not fighting his natural reaction to her nearness. Felicity and arousal went hand in hand. She should be flattered.

"Michael?"

"I'm here." He stroked her hair. As long as he didn't touch the back of her head—or unless she told him otherwise—he figured it was okay.

"When I fell, was it before or after I rolled the ball?"

He vaguely recalled the ball leaving her hand, but whether the sound he remembered was the ball landing or her head, he wasn't positive. But she wanted an answer. "It was after."

"How many pins did I knock down?"

He laughed. "You got a strike, Champ."

"Are you making that up?"

"Yeah."

"That's so sweet." She shifted a little, adjusted her pillow. She rested her arm on his thigh, her fingertips grazing his inseam.

Michael sucked in a breath as she moved her hand over his zipper, then stopped.

"Just checking," she said, sounding satisfied.

"There are assorted descriptive words for women who tease like that."

"Yeah? Like what?"

He liked that there was humor in her voice. She sounded alert and competent. "I'm too much of a gentleman to say them out loud. And you're in no condition to follow through."

"I could be on top."

A laugh burst from him, not just at the suggestion itself, but also at her playful tone of voice. He hadn't expected that. Had she decided to keep him, after all?

"I enjoyed that position," she added.

So had he, but— "We have the rest of our lives, Champ. Try to sleep now."

"Do we, Michael?" Felicity moved back and sat up, which took some effort and his help. She'd been feeling all cozy and warm, but now she didn't. She wanted cozy back, but she also wanted straight answers, the honesty they'd promised each other before. "Have you changed your mind?"

"I haven't changed my mind about anything, Mrs. Fortune."

His reminder that they were married was unnecessary. She didn't forget it for a minute. But was he still not acknowledging that he loved her? Really? Because the way he acted with her seemed loving. Or was she that wrong? Was it just that she was his wife, and that was that?

"Why do the words matter that much?" he asked.

"They just do." She'd heard other women complain now and then that their husbands never said the words and how much that hurt them. Liz had gotten swept into a relationship believing she was loved, then learned not only was she not loved but was also expendable and replaceable. Because he'd never told her he loved her, he figured he hadn't played her false. Wasn't it strange what people considered wasn't a lie?

No matter what promises Michael made about never leaving her, if he didn't love her, why would he stay? Why would she want him to? Why would he be faithful? How could they be happy? Marriage was supposed to be a partnership. If only one person loved—

"I promise I will never leave you," he said, as he had before.

"It's love that gets couples through the trying times that everyone faces, Michael. Love. And a husband and wife who love each other show their children every day in every way what they should be seeking for themselves for a marriage. Did your parents do that? Mine did. That's my example. That's what I want for myself." She was quiet a moment, then added, "Maybe you want what your parents have."

"I don't want to be like my father in any way."

"Why not?" she asked quietly, although she was surprised. "You don't admire him?"

"I admire what he's done, creating a business from just blood, sweat and tears, keeping it a success all these years. But my parents aren't like yours. If they love each other, they don't show it in public. It wasn't my example." His jaw twitched. "You said before that you love me. Do you still?"

"Let me ask you this instead. Are you glad I'm in love with you? Are you glad I told you? Does it make a difference?"

She couldn't read his expression, and suddenly her head began to throb.

"You're in pain," he said, climbing out of bed and heading for the bathroom. "You need to rest, Felicity. We'll talk more in the morning."

She heard him filling a glass. He came back, gave her water and an ibuprofen, which she hoped would take the edge off the throbbing and help her sleep because she had way too much on her mind. She didn't think she could turn off her thoughts.

After downing the pill, she got under the covers again, although she turned her back to him this time. A few minutes later she felt him pull the blankets over her shoulder, then he turned out the light.

Morning would come, their discussion would continue or not. She wondered what his tolerance level would be for more talk, more questions. She'd given him an ultimatum without saying the words *or else*. Would he see it that way?

They were both stubborn. Too stubborn?

She felt herself drifting to sleep. But there he was, inches away, warm, solid and, well, protective. Who would've thought that would be so important to her? Her last thought was how nice it felt to share her bed with him, how easy, how comfortable. She hadn't expected that after sleeping alone all these years.

Chapter Fourteen

"You are not going to work," Michael said the next morning after they left Felicity's doctor's office.

"You were sitting right next to me, Michael. She just cleared me. Bump on the head," Felicity said. "I have none of the symptoms that would keep me resting. My only restriction is that I can't play sports for a week, so, you know. There goes my baseball tryouts."

"Don't joke. I don't care what you call it, you injured your brain."

"I injured my *head*. That's different." He'd dug his heels in, and it was starting to get on her nerves. "I have no products to sell. I have to work today. Period. I'll take it easy. I'll do simple things. Liz will help. I'll hire someone to do the dishes and the heavy lifting."

They reached his car. He opened the door, but before she climbed in, she put a hand on his arm. "Why don't you just go home, Michael? Being here is just agitating you."

"You want me to leave?"

"I have work to do, don't *you?*" She climbed into the car. He didn't quite slam her door shut. She watched him walk in front of the car, saw how his jaw was set.

"We were just starting over," he said after he got in and turned the key.

She heard the hurt in his voice. "I don't have a choice, Michael. I need to work. Surely you understand that."

"I can't keep coming and going, Felicity. I can't keep wondering where I stand."

Felicity rubbed her face with her hands. Already she felt empty inside. She'd known it was coming. Had allowed him back into her life yesterday, hopeful, too hopeful. "I've been as honest as I can be. There's nothing more I can say." *I love you. Why can't you love me back?*

"All right." He pulled away from the curb. "I need to pick up my bag from your apartment, then I'll get out of your life."

The devastation his words struck caught her off guard. She'd thought she was prepared for his going for good. She'd been planning for it mentally. But emotionally? She couldn't have planned for what was hitting her now, having never been in love before. He was going to drive away for good. She was making him leave.

Maybe she *should* accept him on his terms. It was either that or live without him.

No, she was not going to live without hearing words of love, of knowing he was as committed to her as she was to him. She could not do that, no matter how hard it would be to recover. She deserved better.

And if you end up like Liz? No husband ever? No children?

It was unthinkable. She wouldn't be like her aunt. She would put Michael out of her head and open herself to love again. She would.

They didn't speak to each other until they were standing in her bedroom. She didn't know why she followed him up the stairs, and he didn't stop her. They hadn't made the bed. Its rumpled sheets taunted her— they'd slept in the same bed together for the last time.

She watched him pack. He folded everything precisely so, although his movements were stiff. She remembered how he'd taken care of her last night, how gentle he'd been, how his hands had soothed and his voice was tender in the middle of the night each time he woke her.

I love you. Don't go. Fight for me. But the unfair words stuck in her throat.

In the quiet of the room, the clasps on his suitcase sounded like a firing squad.

He didn't look up for several long seconds. When he did, his eyes were distant, as if already disengaged. She didn't want him to leave like that. She wanted him to remember what had been good, that he had been loved.

She moved toward him, twined her arms around his neck and brought herself close. He didn't pull away. She parted her lips, stared at his mouth, saw the moment he gave in. His mouth came down on hers in a long, tender kiss. He dropped his suitcase, slid his arms around her waist, pulled her until their bodies melded.

Her gaze locked with his. "One last time? A final farewell?" she asked.

He almost touched her hair. "Your head."

"We'll be careful." And then she pulled off her blouse.

He laid his hands over her breasts, pressed a kiss to the spot where her bra met in the middle. Her head hurt, but she ignored it. Too much stress, she knew, but not willing to give up this moment.

He pulled her gently to him, tucked her face against his shoulder. "This won't help, Felicity."

Then he picked up his suitcase and left without another word.

She knew he was right. Knew it and hated it.

It was just one more reason to love him for the rest of her life.

The flight from San Antonio seemed to take twelve hours. At first he'd tried to doze, because he'd gotten no rest the night before. None. He'd watched Felicity sleep, was aware of every sound she made, every time she rolled, every fling of her arm, every twitch of her leg.

He'd soothed her through a nightmare, her fingers digging into him, fingernails scraping him. He carried angry red scratches from it. He didn't care then nor now. Badges of honor.

It wasn't even noon, but he ordered a bourbon on ice. The flight attendant was one he'd flown with before a couple of times.

"Rough trip?" she asked as she passed him the drink.

He nodded, not wanting to start a conversation. The drink tasted like kerosene. He set it down hard, too hard, on the tray table, and it spilled, running across the tray onto the floor. The man in the window seat next to him passed Michael his napkins until the attendant noticed and brought a towel.

"Another drink?" she asked.

"No, thanks."

He closed his eyes, but that didn't help at all. He grabbed the in-flight magazine, flipped through the articles without reading anything.

"Woman trouble?" his seatmate asked.

He did not want to talk to anyone. He didn't even want to be polite about it.

"Me, too," the man said, coming to his own conclusion. He held out a hand. "Name's Henry. I just signed divorce papers yesterday." He lifted his glass toward Michael. "She cleaned me out. Left me with a one-bedroom apartment and the kids every other weekend. Not what I expected when I married her." He downed his drink and held up the glass to the flight attendant.

"Did you love her?" The words spilled out of Michael.

"Hell, yeah. At first," Henry added as he was given his second drink. "It gets old in a hurry. You get stuck in a routine. She quit her job when I got transferred, and now, ten years later, she tells me she feels unfulfilled. I thought raising kids was supposed to be the hardest but best job in the world. That's what the women's magazines all say anyway."

Michael didn't want to hear any more. He closed his eyes, ending the conversation. At some point he fell asleep because Henry elbowed him that they were landing.

"Hey, don't listen to me," Henry said. "It's all new and painful. I expect I'll fall in love and get married again. Life goes on, right?"

Which didn't make Michael feel any better.

It was early enough to go to the office, but he went home instead. Everything was closed up. The condo was dark. He didn't turn on any lights nor did he open the blinds. He carried his suitcase into his bedroom and set it on his bed.

He looked around. Like the rest of his place, it was elegantly furnished, with good art he'd picked up himself in his travels, but he couldn't picture Felicity there, not after seeing her bedroom and the kinds of things she surrounded herself with. He opened his suitcase, unpacked by rote, putting his clothes in a laundry bag to be dropped off at the concierge desk. He checked his travel toiletries, refilled his shampoo, put a new blade in his razor, then he stowed the carry-on with his shaving kit in the closet, ready for the next trip.

He changed into workout gear. An hour or two at the gym would take him out of his head. Maybe a massage after, then a power nap.

He pulled open his nightstand drawer to get the key card to the gym. His hand hovered over the open drawer. One of her chocolate mints, the only one he had left, lay there in its True Confections wrapper, daring him to eat it or throw it out.

Michael sat on the side of the bed, never taking his eyes off it. Finally he picked it up and brought it to his nose. He closed his eyes against a rising ache, but saw only images of Felicity—laughing, teasing, concentrating, making love. Lying on the bowling alley floor, not waking up, no matter how many times he shouted her name. Seventy-two seconds, seventy-two years. It seemed the same. He remembered her fighting demons in a nightmare. Asking him for one last time…

He stretched out on his bed, continued to hold the mint under his nose, careful to hang on by its twisted wrapper end. He'd never known a woman like her existed except in the movies, where they were all so perfect.

But she didn't fit here, not in his condo, nor in Atlanta, nor in the life he'd created here. His father had dangled the most tempting carrot of his career, creative control, autonomy, the chance to really lead. He could end up working even longer hours. How could he bring her to that life?

On the other hand, how could he fit in hers?

The ultimate impasse, he thought. There were no answers.

Or were there? Maybe all he had to do was take a page out of Estelle's book and ask. He was done guessing.

Twenty minutes later he rang the bell at his parents' house, knowing his father would be at the office.

"Well, twice in a month. Come in, Michael," his mother said, looking delighted. "May I fix you a drink?"

"I don't want anything, Mom, thanks. I have some

questions I'd like to ask. They're personal, but I hope you'll answer them."

"Of course, darling." They went into the sitting room, her room, a light, airy, yellow space she retreated to in the morning. "I'm all ears."

"Do you love Dad?"

He could see she hadn't expected anything like that, and it felt strange asking, but he'd begun to see he was damaged emotionally, and he wanted to know whether he'd caused it himself or learned it at home.

"I do. Very much."

"Does he love you?"

"Of course he does."

"Does he say so?"

She sat a little straighter, if that was possible. "Not as often as he used to, but that's the way it is after so many years."

"Does it bother you that he doesn't say the words?"

"I can't give you a definitive answer, Michael. Would I like to hear it more often? Yes. But do I think he doesn't love me because he doesn't say it much? No."

Michael leaned toward her, held her gaze. "He's never seemed to treat you…I don't know how to phrase this, but *lovingly* is the word I want to use. I've rarely seen you touch each other or kiss or sit close together on the sofa. The other day in his office I saw you give him a loving look. It took me by surprise because I can't remember seeing it before."

"Maybe you just weren't looking before. Maybe right now you have a particular reason why you're noticing such things. You implied in your father's office that same day that you were having a problem in your relationship with Felicity, but that it was nothing you couldn't handle. I suspect these questions of yours have more to do with you and her than your father and me. Are you looking for someone to blame for your not being, what, emotionally available—isn't that the current phrase being bandied about?"

"Not someone to blame, but a way to open myself up. It's the only way she'll keep me." He realized that sounded pathetic.

"If she's making you work that hard at the relationship, maybe it isn't the right one for you."

"You're prejudiced in my favor."

"Of course I am, darling."

"You would love her." The words came without thought. Why would he think his mother would love Felicity but he couldn't? Awareness started to bring light into his thoughts.

"If you do, I imagine I would, too. Do you love her?"

Michael rolled the words around in his head, as he'd been doing since their wedding night when she'd said the words to him. The light got a little brighter.

He stood. "You've been a big help, Mom."

Looking startled, she stood as well. "I'm always here for you, Michael. I love you very much."

That was it. The key. Apparently some people thought the only way to know for sure that you were loved was if you heard the words. He couldn't remember the last time his mother had told him she loved him. Hearing those words now made him feel like a boy again, safe and secure.

They were just words, but they were the most important words in the human language. As epiphanies went, this was a big one.

Felicity couldn't hide her tears as Sarah-Jane swept into the kitchen at True Confections several days later, then stopped dead in her tracks. "I hate Michael Fortune," Sarah-Jane uttered coldly.

Felicity shook her head again and again. "I was a fool," she said, close to sobbing. "An idiot. An unappreciative dweeb."

"Dweeb?" Sarah-Jane repeated, inching closer to where Felicity rested her elbows against the worktable, her face pressed into her arms. "I don't think dweeb would accurately describe—"

"What*ever*. Womankind should be ashamed of me."

Sarah-Jane pulled up another stool. "What's going on? Did he call?"

"No," Felicity bawled.

"Okay, you're scaring me here, sweetie. What gives?"

"I let him go." She sat up, brushed at her wet cheeks. "He promised me he'd be with me forever, and I told him it wasn't enough. I wanted him to say the words. To tell me he loved me."

"A reasonable expectation."

"But he couldn't do it. He doesn't believe in love. Except that everything he did screamed it to the hills. He was always doing something for me." She began gesturing wildly enough that Sarah-Jane had to pull back. "How many dates did he dream up? Good ones, too. Memorable. Things I'd never done before. He pitched in around here when I needed him—when I didn't even *know* I needed him."

"Did you thank him?"

"Well, of *course* I thanked him. But it was above and beyond. I should've done more for him. He would've done more for *me*. And that night I got hurt at the bowling alley?" She grabbed a fistful of tissues from the box Sarah-Jane offered. "He stayed up all night taking care of me, making sure I was okay. No matter how much I objected to his help, he just kept trying and doing. If that isn't love, I don't know what is."

"Sounds about right to me."

Felicity went silent for a few seconds. "I have to go see him," she said. "Do you think it's too late? I have to tell him it's okay. I don't need the words, not as long as he keeps on showing me he loves me."

She didn't wait for Sarah-Jane's answer. "My suitcase is already packed because I was going to visit my parents. I'll just drive to Atlanta instead. I could be there tomorrow morning. Camp out on his doorstep, if I have to."

"Slow down there, dweeb. You can't drive straight through. You'll have to spend the night along the way. Or take along another driver to share. I'll go with you."

That started a new set of tears, grateful ones. "You're such a great friend." She threw herself into Sarah-Jane's arms.

"Pull yourself together while I go home and pack. Finish up what you're doing, then pick me up." Sarah-Jane looked toward the ceiling and frowned. "That's the second time that plane has flown by so low."

"Probably a crop duster," Felicity said, dabbing her eyes. "It's that time of year."

"Dusting the town? When did we become crops? I'm putting on a gas mask." Instead she went into the coffee shop. A minute later she came back, her eyes wide.

"You need to see this," she said.

"See what? I've got two dozen more pretzels to dip. I can't stop now."

"Yeah, you can. Wash your hands. Come with me."

The plane flew overhead again as Felicity rushed to clean herself up.

A crowd had already gathered on Main Street. The coffee shop had emptied of customers, but people stood in front of every place of business, looking at the sky, holding a hand up to block the sun or just pointing.

"Look," said Sarah-Jane.

The plane came into sight, towing a banner that read, "I Love You. Will You Marry Me?"

Her heart beat loud and fast. "That can't be for me," she said, her throat almost closed. "We're already married. And look, it says I Love You."

"Not many people around here could afford a gesture like that. That's a Fortune scheme. And you know darn well which Fortune."

Felicity looked up and down the street. If it was Michael, he had to be there somewhere—

"Right behind you, Champ."

She whirled around. He looked scared. He looked like he'd slept as little as she had. But his eyes shone with love. Why hadn't she seen that before?

"Felicity Thomas, I lo   "

She put a hand over his mouth. "You don't have to say the words. I know. I *know*. Oh, I have so much to tell you."

He smiled, then got down on one knee and held up a jeweler's box with a diamond engagement ring nestled in it, the stone not ostentatious at all. He knew her well.

"Felicity Thomas," he said in front of everyone, who seemed to be holding their collective breaths. "Will you bring sweetness to my life forever and be my wife?"

She hesitated. They were already married. How could he—

"I've got it all planned out," he said, looking a little desperate when she didn't answer. "We've got an appointment with a Realtor this afternoon to see three houses, and—"

"In Red Rock?" she whispered.

"Yes. I've decided to start a business, probably in San Antonio."

The world had gone quiet as the townspeople tried to listen to their conversation. She grabbed Michael's arm and pulled him into the coffee shop, shutting the door, although they were still on display in the window, which got suddenly crowded.

"Why would you start a new business?" she asked.

"The challenge of creating something myself is appealing, and I don't want to uproot you."

"What if I want to be uprooted?" At his hesitation, she said, "I love Red Rock. I love my business, but this is the right time for me to break out. So this is the critical question, Michael. If location weren't an issue, would you rather start your own business or continue at FortuneSouth?"

"Things are happening in Atlanta. My father is willing to give up some control to me. And honestly, I'd like to see it stay in the family. It's my heritage. It can also be my legacy."

"Then that's what we'll do. Except neither of us will put work above family. I want to travel. I want to have fun."

"Agreed."

"Oh, my gosh, it's driving me crazy, all those people staring at us through the window."

Michael took matters into his own hands. He got down on his knee again. "I didn't ask you the other time. I'm asking now. Will you marry me?"

She wrung her hands. "We're already married."

"They don't know that," he said, hitching his head toward the onlookers. "We'll have a wedding. Your father can beam. Your mother can cry."

"And me?" she asked with tears in her eyes.

"If you must."

She dropped to her knees, wrapped her arms around him and pressed her face into his shoulder.

Michael's heart swelled as he heard her say yes into his shirt. "I don't think everyone else heard you, Champ."

She popped up, rushed to the door, flung it open and yelled, "I told him yes! Yes, yes, yes!"

Then he kissed her in front of the whole town, and they applauded and cheered and elbowed each other. "I told you so" was the phrase Michael could hear most in the din as he slid the ring on her finger.

Sarah-Jane came up and stuffed tissues in her hand, hugged her, then said, "Oh, what the heck," and hugged Michael, too. "If you'd arrived an hour later, we would've been on the road, heading for Atlanta. You didn't stand a chance."

"My heart is so full," Felicity said, leaning against him.

"I know what you mean." He cupped her neck and drew her to him, kissing her hard and long. Ahh, there it was. Mint and chocolate. His world was aligned again. "I lo—"

Again she put her hand over his mouth.

"Do you plan on doing that ten times a day for the next seventy years?" he asked, smiling but also curious why she wasn't letting him say it.

"I figured it out, Michael. I came to realize that words don't matter. Action does."

"I figured it out, too," he said, stroking her hair. "It wasn't that I didn't believe in love but that until I met you, I didn't understand it. Love isn't one thing. It's everything. It can't be separated from all the other elements that make a relationship work. It can't *be* on its own. That's why I didn't get it. I thought it was something separate."

"And I'd felt the opposite," she said. "I thought one thing was more important than the others. It's not. You're right. It's not its own thing. It's part of something larger."

"Well, look at us. Modern-day philosophers." Smiling, he put a hand over her mouth and said, "I love you, Mrs. Fortune. And I'd like to see the world through your eyes."

"Two pairs of rose-colored glasses coming up."

Michael smiled at her enthusiasm. Now his life would really begin. All because of a quaint little town called Red Rock.

* * * * *

*Look for the next installment
in the new Special Edition continuity*
THE FORTUNES OF TEXAS: SOUTHERN INVASION
*When single father Asher Fortune relocates to Red
Rock, all he hopes to find is some peace of mind—
and a good home for his young son. But little Jace
thinks his new nanny would make a perfect mommy,
and when this mischievous little boy decides to play
matchmaker, anything can happen!*
Don't miss
A SMALL FORTUNE
by Marie Ferrarella
On sale March 2013,
wherever Harlequin Books are sold.

REQUEST YOUR FREE BOOKS!

2 FREE NOVELS PLUS 2 FREE GIFTS!

(H) HARLEQUIN®

SPECIAL EDITION

Life, Love & Family

YES! Please send me 2 FREE Harlequin® Special Edition novels and my 2 FREE gifts (gifts are worth about $10). After receiving them, if I don't wish to receive any more books, I can return the shipping statement marked "cancel." If I don't cancel, I will receive 6 brand-new novels every month and be billed just $4.49 per book in the U.S. or $5.24 per book in Canada. That's a savings of at least 14% off the cover price! It's quite a bargain! Shipping and handling is just 50¢ per book in the U.S. and 75¢ per book in Canada.* I understand that accepting the 2 free books and gifts places me under no obligation to buy anything. I can always return a shipment and cancel at any time. Even if I never buy another book, the two free books and gifts are mine to keep forever.

235/335 HDN FVTV

Name	(PLEASE PRINT)	
Address		Apt. #
City	State/Prov.	Zip/Postal Code

Signature (if under 18, a parent or guardian must sign)

Mail to the **Harlequin® Reader Service:**
IN U.S.A.: P.O. Box 1867, Buffalo, NY 14240-1867
IN CANADA: P.O. Box 609, Fort Erie, Ontario L2A 5X3

Want to try two free books from another line?
Call 1-800-873-8635 or visit www.ReaderService.com.

* Terms and prices subject to change without notice. Prices do not include applicable taxes. Sales tax applicable in N.Y. Canadian residents will be charged applicable taxes. Offer not valid in Quebec. This offer is limited to one order per household. Not valid for current subscribers to Harlequin Special Edition books. All orders subject to credit approval. Credit or debit balances in a customer's account(s) may be offset by any other outstanding balance owed by or to the customer. Please allow 4 to 6 weeks for delivery. Offer available while quantities last.

Your Privacy—The Harlequin® Reader Service is committed to protecting your privacy. Our Privacy Policy is available online at www.ReaderService.com or upon request from the Harlequin Reader Service.

We make a portion of our mailing list available to reputable third parties that offer products we believe may interest you. If you prefer that we not exchange your name with third parties, or if you wish to clarify or modify your communication preferences, please visit us at www.ReaderService.com/consumerchoice or write to us at Harlequin Reader Service Preference Service, P.O. Box 9062, Buffalo, NY 14269. Include your complete name and address.

HSE13

*In Buckshot Hills, Texas, a sexy doctor meets his match
in the least likely woman—a beautiful cowgirl looking to
reinvent herself….*

Enjoy a sneak peek from USA TODAY *bestselling author
Judy Duarte's new Harlequin® Special Edition® story,*
TAMMY AND THE DOCTOR *,the first book in
Byrds of a Feather, a brand-new miniseries launching
in March 2013!*

***

Before she could comment or press Tex for more details, a
couple of light knocks sounded at the door.

Her grandfather shifted in his bed, then grimaced. "Who
is it?"

"Mike Sanchez."

Doc? Tammy's heart dropped to the pit of her stomach
with a thud, then thumped and pumped its way back up
where it belonged.

"Come on in," Tex said.

Thank goodness her grandfather had issued the invitation, because she couldn't have squawked out a single word.

As Doc entered the room, looking even more handsome
than he had yesterday, Tammy struggled to remain cool and
calm.

And it wasn't just her heartbeat going wacky. Her feminine hormones had begun to pump in a way they'd never
pumped before.

"Good morning," Doc said, his gaze landing first on Tex,
then on Tammy.

As he approached the bed, he continued to look at Tammy,

his head cocked slightly.

"What's the matter?" she asked.

"I'm sorry. It's just that your eyes are an interesting shade of blue. I'm sure you hear that all the time."

"Not really." And not from anyone who'd ever mattered. In truth, they were a fairly common color—like the sky or bluebonnets or whatever. "I've always thought of them as run-of-the-mill blue."

"There's nothing ordinary about it. In fact, it's a pretty shade."

The compliment set her heart on end. But before she could think of just the perfect response, he said, "If you don't mind stepping out of the room, I'd like to examine your grandfather."

Of course she minded leaving. She wanted to stay in the same room with Doc for the rest of her natural-born days. But she understood her grandfather's need for privacy.

"Of course." Apparently it was going to take more than simply batting her eyes to woo him, but there was no way Tammy would be able to pull off a makeover by herself. Maybe she could ask her beautiful cousins for help?

She had no idea what to say the next time she ran into them. But somehow, by hook or by crook, she'd have to think of something.

Because she was going to risk untold humiliation and embarrassment by begging them to turn a cowgirl into a lady!

***

*Look for TAMMY AND THE DOCTOR from
Harlequin® Special Edition® available March 2013*

SPECIAL EDITION

Life, Love and Family

Coming in March 2013 from fan-favorite author

KATHLEEN EAGLE

Cowboy Jack McKenzie has a checkered past,
but when rancher's daughter Lily reluctantly visits her
father, he wants more than anything to show that
he's a reformed man. Has she made up her mind too
early that this would be a short stay at the ranch?

Look for *One Less Lonely Cowboy* next month from Kathleen Eagle.

*Available March 2013 from Harlequin Special Edition
wherever books are sold.*